THE MYSTERY OF SEAL ISLANDS

Airplane Girls #3

By **Harrison Bardwell**

(Originally published 1931)

. . . .

TABLE OF CONTENTS

THROUGH THE STORM

CHAPTER I
A BITTER BLOW

"I say, Berta, thought you were going to do some work for that Mr. Howe of the Federal Service. Did it fall through?"

"Haven't heard much more about it, Harv," Roberta answered her brother, as she poured maple syrup over a serving of piping hot pancakes. Her mother came in at that moment with a replenished bowl of oatmeal, and she paused with an anxious glance at her young daughter.

"Hope you do not hear anything more about it, dear. I feel that your activities in helping clear up the mystery at Lurtiss Field placed you in any number of very dangerous situations. Being a pilot is hazardous enough without adding to the difficulties by running down air-gangsters of any kind," she said soberly.

"Perhaps Mr. Howe has discovered that he does not require your services. In work of that nature very often, when men on the job think they have struck a hard snag, something comes up suddenly which clears the matter so they do not require outside assistance," remarked Mr. Langwell, then smiled at his wife. "As a maker of pancakes, my dear, you draw first prize. The only drawback to such a breakfast is a man's limited capacity."

"You aren't announcing that you have been limiting yourself!" Roberta laughed.

"No, that isn't my claim, but I have to confess that my limit is in sight," he told her.

"Tough luck, Dad. Now, I am only getting well started," Roberta said, then added to her mother, "If you drew prizes for all the good things you cook you would have to have a museum for them as large as Colonel Lindbergh's in St. Louis."

"Second the motion," Harvey put in, then went on to his young sister, "Who's the lady you have been piloting along the coast the last couple of weeks? Larry Kingsley told me she's got loads of money and has taken to taxiing about in the air with no particular objective."

"Oh, that is Mrs. Pollzoff. Her husband used to be in the fur business and when he died she sold her interest to a big syndicate, she told me, because she knew there wasn't much chance of her making a success against such competition. She is keen on aviation, and bought herself a plane but has never been able to get a license. I asked Mr. Trowbridge and he said he thought it was because she showed very little judgment in an emergency; she cracked-up three times, and they forbade her to fly alone."

"I should think they would," Mrs. Langwell exclaimed indignantly.

"That's all I know about her, except that she is madder than a dozen wet hens at the government for depriving her of the right to fly; and she seems to be interested in fishes."

"Fishes?"

"Yes. She always carries a wonderful pair of glasses, and when we are over the water orders that I fly low and as slowly as possible while she examines the deep. I have to keep my eyes on the board, so I haven't been able to look at what attracts her attention especially, but a couple of times she has seemed very pleased over what she examined, and appears to admire the schools of fish we have followed a couple of times. Guess it's a hobby of hers, and she hasn't anything special to do, so she rides it—"

"Or rides the air," Harvey laughed.

"Are you children riding in with me?" Mr. Langwell asked. "The time is getting short."

"I am, Dad, thanks. If you will take me as far as the subway in Jamaica, I'll land just in time for class," Harvey answered.

"Phil will be here to pick me up, thank you," Roberta replied, so, as the meal was finished, and the last pancake had disappeared, they left the table to start on the day's occupations. Harvey raced up the stairs, three at a jump, while his sister gave her mother a hand straightening the dining room as she waited for Phil Fisher to take her to the flying field.

"I hear the motor, my dear," Mrs. Langwell interrupted. "You'd better hurry."

"He's early this morning, but probably he has something to do before schedule." The girl hastened with her own preparations so that when the young man appeared at the door she was properly helmeted and all ready to take the air.

"Top of the morning to you," Phil called cheerily. "Your esteemed passenger wants to make an early start, so the boys will have Nike warmed up for you and you can start as soon as you get to the field."

"It's mighty good of you to come and fetch me," Roberta smiled at the president's son, who had not so many weeks before gone through a series of exciting, dangerous air-adventures with her. But those things were all in the day's work and belonged to the past; the new day awaited them.

"It isn't much of a hop, and as Mrs. Pollzoff has all the earmarks of being a good customer, she must be humored," Phil grinned. "Just the same, I'm glad they wished her on you and Nike instead of the Moth and yours truly."

"Well, it's no particular fun piloting her. I wish she'd decide she wants variety, and give you all a chance at the job," Roberta told him. They were making their way to where the Moth, Phil's own imported machine, waited to leap in the air with them. "I say, when is Mr. Howe going to start that investigation he spoke of a few weeks ago. Heard anything about it?"

"You are not so fed up on Mrs. Pollzoff that you want to get away from us all, are you?" he demanded.

"No, of course not, but I was wondering what his plan was and what happened to it, if anything," Roberta answered.

"Glad to hear you do not want to leave. Gosh, to lose our only girl sky-pilot would be—unthinkable; but, come to think of it, Howe came to the house to see Dad one day last week, perhaps they are getting it fixed up for you to take on the job. I heard the Old Man say the Federal representative would be at the office today, so perhaps you'll get some information. Here we are." They reached the plane and Roberta climbed into the seat beside the pilot's, adjusted straps and parachute, while the young man gave his machine a thorough looking-over then took his own place.

"Any idea what it's all about?"

"A small one. Several governments—ours and a couple of others, are trying to trace down illegal seal fishing; catch the lads who don't follow the rules. Contact." They were off, and Roberta inquired no more about the government work because Phil's account of it sounded quite as tame as piloting Mrs. Pollzoff. Presently the Moth dropped out of the sky, landed near the office of the Lurtiss Airplane Company and a bit later the girl sky-pilot presented herself at the private office of Mr.

Trowbridge for whom she worked when she first joined the organization as a secretary. Mr. Wallace, one of the special instructors, was already there, and when Roberta entered, they both rose to their feet to wish her good morning.

"Anything special?" she asked when greetings were exchanged.

"Only Mrs. Pollzoff. She ought to be here any minute," Mr. Trowbridge replied.

"Howe is coming in this morning," Mr. Wallace added.

"Phil told me—"

"Yes, and here I am," Mr. Howe announced himself as he entered. "They told me you were all in here, so I took the liberty of coming in without knocking; I can go out the same way if you like."

"You can stay here, without knocking," Mr. Trowbridge hastened to assure him. "I'm thinking Miss Langwell is glad to see you."

"She has been handling a job that is dull as ditch-water," Wallace put in quickly.

"She will not find my work dull, but it will be cold, for it may take her to the Bering Sea," Mr. Howe informed them. "I expect to be ready for her soon."

"It sounds no end exciting," Roberta said and her eyes sparkled. A job that would take her to the Bering Sea appeared to have endless possibilities and she was keenly interested. Just then the phone rang and Mr. Trowbridge answered it.

"Your passenger has arrived," he told Roberta.

"I'll go right down."

"See you later," Mr. Howe called after her as she hurried away. Ten minutes later Nike, her own prize plane, was taxied to the edge of the field, where Roberta and her passenger, a tall, slender woman, whose flying costume, however, gave her huge proportions, waited. The machine came up just as Mr. Wallace and Mr. Howe, in the company's carrying automobile started for the further end of the field.

"There is to be a test for the racing machines this evening, Miss Langwell," the instructor called as he brought the car to a stop close to where the two were standing. Roberta noticed that the Federal man gave her companion a swift, all-inclusive glance, but since that was the way with Mr. Howe, and he always looked everybody up and down, she did not think anything about it.

"Hope I can watch it," she replied.

"All set, Miss Langwell." Nike came to a stop a few yards away, so, forgetting everything else, Roberta turned her whole attention to the task at hand. Presently all was ready, and in another moment, Nike was leaping into the air, carrying her pilot and passenger up a steep climb until they were well in the air, then her nose was leveled and she shot east and south, as Mrs. Pollzoff designated the direction she wished to take.

Having taken the woman every day for over two weeks, Roberta knew pretty well how high and fast she preferred to travel, so they did not waste any time on discussions, but shot ahead swiftly. Almost as soon as she was seated, Mrs. Pollzoff got the powerful field glasses out of their case, and as soon as they were over the water, trained them on its smooth surface. The day was clear, the sky blue, and the sea calm, so the task of piloting was not arduous, and Roberta let her mind wander on speculations about her companion. That the woman was wealthy was obvious, but for the first time the girl began to wonder about her interest in things in the ocean. It occurred to her that the woman might be looking for sunken vessels, or something of that nature, but she had never let a word drop regarding what she sought. Then it struck Roberta that she was a bit mysterious. Although it wasn't necessary for passengers to explain their businesses or hobbies, still when anyone traveled day after day with the same pilot it was only natural that they should establish more or less friendly relations and exchange odds and ends about each other. Thinking it over carefully, the girl realized that except for the facts that Mrs. Pollzoff's husband had come to the United States from Russia when he was a lad, that he had gone into the fur business, and had been dead two years, she knew nothing more than the bit of information gleaned in the office regarding the failure to pass the flying tests to fly her own machine.

"Follow the coast south and keep outside the Government limit," Mrs. Pollzoff directed after they had been in the air about an hour. "Have you plenty of gas? I want to remain up several hours."

"Plenty," Roberta assured her but she was becoming really puzzled about her passenger. It could not be possible that Mrs. Pollzoff was in search of vessels carrying liquor, for she never showed the slightest interest in ships of any description when they were sighted, but this was the first time she expressed a desire to keep beyond the jurisdiction of the United States. The request was strange and the girl pilot felt oddly disturbed by it.

But if Mrs. Pollzoff was doing anything forbidden by the laws of the United States, she gave no sign of it during the hours which followed. Her glasses swept the water as they had every other day, and if she noticed the ships, large or small, plowing through them, she was remarkably successful in keeping the fact to herself. Except for her usual directions regarding the course they were to follow, she said nothing more; and at noon she signified her desire to return to land. She requested that they come down on the southern part of New Jersey, but here she merely led the way to a restaurant where she ordered lunch for both of them.

Seated across from her, Roberta noted that she might be about thirty-five years old, and her mouth, which was rather large, was set firmly, like a mask. Without consulting her companion, she ordered an excellent meal, and after the first course was set before them, her face relaxed somewhat, as if she suddenly realized her duties as a hostess.

"You are an excellent pilot, Miss Langwell," she remarked. There was a musical quality to her voice, as if she might sing a good contralto, and when her eyes softened it gave her features an expression of real charm.

"Thank you," Roberta replied, a bit at a loss. Since she had started to wonder about her passenger a feeling of awkwardness came over her, and she flushed with embarrassment.

"There is little money these days in commercial piloting, I am informed," Mrs. Pollzoff went on in a chatty sort of fashion as if she were filling in the gap with small talk.

"I like the work," the girl answered.

"You doubtless have many passengers and various experiences?"

"I guess we all do," Roberta replied. Something inside her warned her that perhaps it would be just as well if she did not become too confidential over her work. Since she had won her own license she had learned much about human nature, and every day she was adding to that store of knowledge, either through her own experiences or those of her co-pilots, so her bump of caution was developing rapidly.

"Ah, the waiter." The man appeared and the meal was eaten almost in silence. Twice Roberta tried to break the awkwardness of the situation, but the replies from her companion were the briefest possible, so she gave up the attempt after the second failure. She was glad when the meal was over and they returned to Nike. They took their places and several times during the return trip, the pilot saw her companion give her short quick glances.

There was something about Mrs. Pollzoff which made Roberta recall the time Phil had been employed to take an old man on regular trips to Philadelphia. Young Fisher had described his passenger as "falling to pieces," but after a number of trips, Roberta had chanced to see the pair in the air; the ancient man pressing a pistol to the back of his pilot's head. It wasn't a pleasant memory, in fact it added greatly to the girl's uneasiness, but, if her companion's intention was evil, she gave no evidence of it. They reached the field in good time without mishap, and as soon as they were out of the cockpit, the passenger turned for an instant.

"Tomorrow I shall come at the same time."

"Let them know at the office," Roberta replied mechanically. Just at that moment Phil's Moth came roaring over the field and lighted close by. He waved to Roberta, who waited for him.

"Have a wild time?"

"Wild as a plate of soup." Roberta told him how she had spent the hours and what had been passing through her mind. They walked slowly toward the office and Phil listened thoughtfully.

"Wonder what her game is anyway? I'm going to tell Trowbridge to have some—"

"I say, Kingsley." Someone called the president's son, and with a nod to his companion, he strode off to see what was wanted.

Roberta proceeded, but as she went she wished she had not spoken to Phil of her nervousness. Probably it was just silly and she certainly didn't want to be relieved of the responsibility because she was afraid. After all, there wasn't a thing in the world to be afraid of, nothing but a collection of wild guesses. It was unlike the time the "old man" had tried to appropriate the Moth, for then the country was filled with horrible stories of "Blue Air-pirates," but now everything was as it should be. In fact, life was a bit dull except for the unending joy of racing into the sky. By that time she reached Mr. Trowbridge's office, but as she opened the door she heard Mr. Wallace saying angrily, "Well, I'll be darned if I see it. Oh, oh, hello Miss

Langwell." With that he rushed out of the room and banged the door so hard that it jarred the place.

"Oh, er, oh," Mr. Trowbridge glanced at her, then began to fumble with some papers on his desk. "Wallace is a bit upset, you'll have to excuse him."

"Sorry if I interrupted—"

"Er, no, you didn't. That is, well, you have to be told—"

"Is something wrong, Mr. Trowbridge?" she asked quietly.

"Well, er, yes there is—"

"Anything happened to Mother or—"

"Oh, no, what a blundering ass I am; but, you know, it's this way, the stock market—well, you've heard how it broke a lot of people. We have to—er, reduce expenses, er, you see— there was a meeting, and some of the pilots have to go—I'm sorry, hate to lose you, hate it like fury, and so does Wallace."

CHAPTER 11
ANOTHER HARD BLOW

After making this astonishing statement, Mr. Trowbridge walked hastily to the window and ran his fingers around his collar as if it was tight. For a moment Roberta stood in her tracks, her helmet shoved back off her forehead, her wavy hair falling in unruly twists, while her eyes stared at the man's back so hard they finally forced him to turn around.

"Oh, I say, Miss Langwell—" he paused, then walked briskly to his desk, cleared his throat, opened and closed a drawer, and without looking at her again, spoke with an effort. "I'm sorry about this—" he got up again, "but, don't take it so hard. You've got one of the best records of any pilot in the country, you own Nike, and you are sure to pick up something quickly."

"I, I wasn't thinking of that," she managed to answer. It was her first position since she had been graduated from business school, so of course it was the first time she had lost one, and now it swept over her, like an on-rushing tide, that she was outside of the organization; she was no longer a part of the Lurtiss Airplane Company. She swallowed, bravely endeavoring to buck up or snap out of her depression, but it wasn't easy.

"No, surely you weren't. Sit down a moment and collect yourself. This financial mess is likely to adjust itself overnight, then the whole works will be booming again. It can't be anything more than temporary, and in a few weeks you'll be back again. You'll be the first one recalled, for your service has been excellent, excellent."

"Thank you so much, Mr. Trowbridge—"

"There's a lot of pick-up work. Odds and ends; people hiring planes for trips and business purposes. With Nike you can find plenty to do. If I may make a suggestion, I'd say do some of that sort of thing temporarily—but—then," he glanced at her and frowned. "You probably won't want to see one of us again, ever—"

"I'll be glad to come back whenever you have a place for me," she told him hastily. Mr. Trowbridge was feeling so miserable that Roberta was sorry for him and tried to cheer him up.

"That's great. Knew you were not the sore-head kind. You can understand how things will happen—"

"I guess I don't very well, but I am sure you have all been most kind to me. I'd rather be dismissed because of reducing expenses than because I didn't do my job well. Mr. Howe was in this morning. Did he say anything about the work he wanted done?"

"Well, er, he did mention it, but I believe he left for Washington and I don't know when he'll be back. He can get your address from us any time he wants it, or you could send him a note—"

"Guess I won't do that, but I will leave the address, thank you." She wrote it down for him and was glad to be able to do something for a moment. "If he wants me he can find me easily enough. You have been mighty kind—I'm wondering if—if it will seem—that is, I wish you would tell the others that I appreciate—I—somehow I don't feel exactly like saying goodbye to them—"

"I'll be glad to. They will understand." Mr. Trowbridge answered so quickly that she was a little startled at his readiness, but that, too, passed out of her mind immediately.

"I'll get Nike—"

"One of the boys will fix her up for you, and any time you want her given an overhauling, drop down here. She'll be taken care of the same as usual; we'd feel neglected if you did not permit us to do that for you." He tried to smile, but the effort was not much of a success.

"Thank you—" Quickly she faced about and hurried out of the office, closing the door after her much more softly than Mr. Wallace had done a few minutes before. She did not notice as she made her way to the big entrance, but before she got half way to the hangar, she met Phil.

"Oh, here you are, say" he stopped short. "What's the matter, Roberta, you look as if you'd seen a ghost!"

"I'm all right," she answered and blinked furiously.

"Where you going?" demanded Phil.

"Home."

"Let me take you." He swung in beside her.

"Thank you, I'm going alone—Oh, it's all right, I mean I'm all right, but, well, Mr. Trowbridge just told me about the—"

"About the what?"

"He told me the firm has to let some of its pilots go, and I am one of them." Phil stopped short, caught her arm and swung her around so that she faced him.

"What the heck are you talking about?" he demanded.

"I just lost my job and I guess I am making an awful boob of myself." She forced her lips into a good imitation of a smile.

"I say, you are full of—quit kidding—"

"I am not kidding, Phil."

"You mean to say Trowbridge just told you that you can't work here any more," he persisted.

"Yes I do," she answered. "So long, Phil."

"I say, wait a minute, while I look into this," he called, but a plane was roaring onto the field and the noise of the motor drowned his voice so the girl did not hear. Her throat choked as she hurried to get away, and after staring at her a few minutes, young Fisher, his forehead puckered in a deep frown, strode toward the office, and met Trowbridge just coming out. "What's the big idea?" he demanded.

"You mean about Miss Langwell?"

"Of course," Phil snapped.

"Howe has some sort of idea that he wants to put into operation. He believes that it will help him capture a choice collection of bandits and he thinks some of them will make use of Miss Langwell, so she's in the Government employ really, but she doesn't know it."

"It sounds blamed putrid to me," Phil declared, and he started down the steps.

"Give it a trial, Phil, for it's a whale of a thing," the man urged. "We don't any of us think much of the plan, but she promised to help him and probably his way is best."

"Well—" Just then the familiar roar of Nike's engine announced that their Girl Sky Pilot was on her way home, and if Roberta could have had an inkling of that conversation, it would have brightened the outlook of everything for weeks to come. But she was blissfully unconscious that she was playing a part, and life seemed to be of the deepest indigo.

It took Nike only a short time to get her young owner home and to her own new hangar. The Langwells lived on the outskirts of one of Long Island's many small towns, east of the flying field on a part of an ancient farm. There were several acres in the property and since they had become interested in aviation, Harvey and his sister had built a house for their planes out of an old barn. They had smoothed off a fair runway, not as good, of course, as those on the regulation fields, but it was fairly smooth and perfectly safe for landing and taking-off. Nike was brought down in a perfect three-point and mechanically the girl glanced at the wind-sock fluttering under the old weather-cock.

There was a catch in the girl's throat when she unlocked the long sliding doors and assured herself that her brother's plane, the Falcon, which that young man rarely used since he was back at college, was properly placed so her own machine could be run in easily. While she was attending to the task she heard the house door open, and realized that her mother was probably coming out to learn why she was home so early. With a determined effort she shook off the gloom, or at least its outward appearance, so when Mrs. Langwell appeared she was greeted by a smiling young daughter.

"'Lo, Mummy," she called.

"All right, my dear?"

"Top hole. As soon as I lock the door I'll be in with you," she answered with a disarming cheeriness.

"May I help?"

"Sure, tell me if I'm getting too close to the Falcon's wings."

"You have plenty of space." Presently the two machines were locked in to exchange confidences if they felt so disposed, while Roberta and her mother walked arm in arm to the house. "I suppose you have to take someone in the morning and that is why you have brought Nike home for a visit."

"No, that's a wrong guess, Mummy." They went into the house and Mrs. Langwell glanced anxiously at the girl.

"Sure you are all right, dear?"

"Fine as silk. Fact is, Mummy, the stock-market slump has hit some of our directors, hard, and the company has to reduce expenses. Mr. Trowbridge told me when I came back with my passenger this afternoon."

"The stock-market slump; why, that was months ago!"

"I don't know much about it except what I heard you and Dad saying last fall. Is it possible that it still affects business?" Roberta didn't ask because she was at all interested in the "Bulls and Bears of Wall Street," but just for the sake of talking. She removed her flying coat and hat and hung them, with a sigh, in the hall closet, wondering a bit sadly how soon she would use them again. She knew that she simply couldn't leave the beloved Nike idle in the hangar; she would certainly take it out for pleasure, but that was different from being really a part of the great force of men and women aiding in the world's grand and almost brand new industry.

"Probably," her mother answered. "Your father was saying only a few nights ago that a good many big business men have gone on with their projects confident that the financial situation would improve, but while it is getting better, the growth is slow and any number of them have had to drop out."

"Dad didn't get hit, did he?"

"No dear, he has some stock in various concerns but it is not the kind that fluctuates with an erratic market."

"Mr. Trowbridge suggested that I pick up some odds and ends for a while and probably in a few weeks things will be better with the company and I can go back. He was sort of shot up when he told me," Roberta explained.

"I'll be mighty glad to have my girl home with me for a while," Mrs. Langwell smiled.

"And it will not be hard on my own feelings, to stay," she laughed. "I've been thinking I may go in for some record-breaking flights—"

"My dear—" her mother protested.

"I don't mean stunts; just long distance hops."

"But will Nike carry gas enough for trips?"

"She'll go a lot, Mummy. You know Nike has been a sort of pet of Mr. Wallace's and he's put all sorts of improvements into her. She's a top-notch bird and no one except us and a few men in the company really know how capable she is, and we're not telling."

"Suppose you stay home for a day or two anyway before you fly off from the nest, Honey," her mother pleaded.

"All right. Tell you what, I'll take you joy-riding around the skies," she promised and although Mrs. Langwell made no objection and fully appreciated that flying was a splendid means of travel, she just could not think of herself as a successful joy-rider.

That evening when Mr. Langwell reached home he heard the news with some surprise and questioned Roberta closely. However, he did not make any guesses and did his best to cheer her up.

"You have been most fortunate, my dear, as a young business woman, and this is the first time you have lost a position, so it seems more tragic than anything else in the world, but as you gain experience you will understand that almost any enterprise has its ups and downs, the downs often being in the majority. Sudden changes are frequently necessary. Just figure up your assets; you have Nike, an A-One license, know how to be a good secretary in case you cannot get a pilot's berth, some money in the savings bank—"

"And health," her mother added.

"And the best family in the world," Roberta laughed. "My goodness, when I come to count my blessings they mount up to the skies, almost."

"That's the way to look at it," her father encouraged. "Life is not all a path of roses, and sometimes even the roses have thorns. When things run along too smoothly one gets careless and unprepared to face the rough places."

"Guess it is like flying," Roberta answered. "You have to keep alert for the pockets, bumps, and cliffs, besides watching the machinery, if you don't want a smash."

"That's the idea. I know your mother will be happy if you remain grounded for a while, and I am sure that if I try hard, I can bear up under it," he grinned mischievously.

"Dad, you are a fraud," the girl laughed heartily.

"As long as my efforts are not flat tires I'll survive that," he retorted, and after that the fact that she had lost her position was dismissed, the three spent a thoroughly enjoyable evening. Before she hopped into bed that night, Roberta glanced at the converted hangar and couldn't suppress a little sigh.

"As a good sport, I am something of a flat tire myself," she said softly and was about to turn away from the window when she thought she caught sight of something moving slowly along the door. Instantly forgetting sleepiness she stared hard for fully a minute until she convinced herself that there was something there. "It may be a dog," she told herself, for although the Langwells didn't have one, most of the neighbors did, and at night the beasts were given to prowling about the community.

Watching a bit longer the girl came to the conclusion that if it was a dog the beast was behaving oddly. She didn't recall ever seeing one move so stealthily. She reasoned that it might be getting ready to pounce on something, but in the darkness she couldn't see a thing it could be after. If it was a man, a prowler, what was he doing near the hangar? Her heart leaped to her throat as she thought of Nike poised inside beside the Falcon, but certainly no one would dream of trying to steal the ancient plane belonging to her brother, for its days of usefulness were practically over. Yet, she was sure that no one knew that her own prize machine rested behind that door. The huddled bunch of blackness moved forward, gave a little leap, and she leaned over the sill.

"Sure, it's a dog. Probably one of the big ones on a neighborly tour of investigation." She watched a bit longer, and was just about to get into bed when she spied a thin streak of light, like a carefully shaded flash, that cast a faint glow on the ground. Then it began to travel swiftly up toward the lock and to her straining ears came the faintest sound of scraping. Quick as a thought Roberta threw on a robe, jammed her feet into her slippers as she hurried across the room, then raced to her Father's door, where she knocked.

"Dad, dad," she called softly.

"My dear, what is the matter?" Mrs. Langwell had heard and leaped out of bed in fright before her husband was fully awake. Her hand moved along the wall for the electric switch, but Roberta placed her own over it quickly.

"Don't, Mummy," she whispered.

"What is the matter, Berta?" her father asked. He was wide awake now and up beside her. "Are you sick?"

"No, Dad, but someone is trying to get into the hangar!"

"To get into the hangar?"

"Yes, I saw someone moving by the door and watched it. Thought it was a dog, then whoever it is turned on a little light by the opening," she explained excitedly.

"No one would try to steal the planes, either of them, dear, it would make too much noise," he protested.

"If they get the door open they could muffle the machine a bit, roll it out and get away," she insisted.

"That is so," he admitted.

"They would not have to take it far before they start the engine, then they can get off in it. Nike doesn't need any warming up—"

"That's so. Come into your room." The adults' own sleeping quarters did not face the rear, so the old barn could not be seen or watched from their windows.

"You must be careful, both of you," Mrs. Langwell urged anxiously.

"We will." He had already gotten into his own shoes, which he did not stop to tie, while his wife handed him his bath robe, which was dark colored and warm.

"Come along." The pair, with Mrs. Langwell following in the distance, proceeded quickly. In a moment they were at the window, and there was no doubting the fact that prowlers of some kind were working to open the door. The light shone in a faint round circle over the lock, and a figure, which looked tall and grotesque, was busy with a tool. So far as they could see, only one person was at the hangar but they were reasonably sure that at least one guard was on duty to warn the robber if necessary.

"I'm going out——." Mr. Langwell caught her quickly.

"Do nothing of the kind," he ordered firmly. "Get me that old shotgun out of the closet. Be careful of it."

"All right." She flew swiftly to the place where her father stored all sorts of odds and ends, including an ancient double-barreled shotgun which had been one of his treasures when he was a young man. Since the children had grown up it had been kept loaded and both of them had been taught how to handle it without danger. Quickly Roberta took it from its hooks and hurried back to her father.

"Thank you. Stand back." He rested the long barrel on the sill, the sight trained on the barn, then, without an unnecessary sound, he pulled the trigger, first one, then the other. There was a loud report, followed instantly by a hail of lead which crackled as it spattered over a wide surface.

CHAPTER III
A STRANGE PROPOSAL

Simultaneously with the sound of peppering bullets came a furious string of oaths. A second figure leaped from the corner of the old building and then the gun spoke again. This time, amid the hail of small bullets came a muffled cry of pain, subdued curses, and a swift scrambling of two pairs of feet taking their owners helter-skelter from the vicinity. From a distance came the roar of a motor thrown open quickly somewhere down the road, a clutch released as if by frantic hands, then an automobile in motion, but moving slowly.

"Nipped them," Dad declared with satisfaction.

"Wish you could have done more than that," Roberta said without any compunction.

"At any rate, they are frightened away. Turn on the lights, Mother, please, and we'll do some investigating." Mrs. Langwell pressed the switches which immediately illuminated the whole house, and the sounds of shouts came from the home of the nearest neighbors. This was taken up by other persons, while someone on a motorcycle seemed to turn as if giving chase after the robbers.

"Don't go out," Mrs. Langwell urged as her husband began to don his trousers hastily under his robe.

"It's quite safe," he assured her. Before he was ready there came a pounding at the door—alarmed voices shouted, "You people all right, Langwell?"

"That's Mr. Howard. He's the sheriff of the county and must have been in the neighborhood."

"I'll be right down," Mrs. Langwell called. Presently the officer of the law was standing in the hall, while she explained what had happened.

"Glad nobody's hurt, least-wise, none of you folks. I'll go out and have a look around." There was a business-like gun in his hand and his chin was set firmly.

"I'm coming with you," Mr. Langwell called from the top of the stairs as he hurried to join the sheriff.

"I'm coming too, Dad."

"Stay with your mother, please," he answered, so Roberta obeyed.

"There isn't a thing you can do out there, Honey," Mrs. Langwell assured her. "And you might get in the way."

So the girl had to be content to remain inside, while sounds of people running, sharp questions, brief answers, and the noise of automobiles stopping while the occupants demanded to know what was the difficulty came to them from outside. Half an hour later Mr. Langwell came back with the sheriff and their nearest neighbor, and although they were greatly excited, they had discovered nothing more than some footprints of the robbers, and the place where a large car had been parked by the side of the road, obviously waiting to assist the thieves in their enterprise, or get them away from the scene of their mischief.

"That's a good lock you have on the building," the sheriff announced. "Kept them from opening the door right away."

"Mighty good thing your daughter happened to look out of her window before she turned in to bed," remarked the neighbor.

"Yes, indeed it is."

"I call the best part that you had a pop-gun to pepper them with. I heard one cry out, and from my window I saw that the fellow hiding nearest the barn grabbed toward his face."

"From that window of yours you must have had a pretty good look at them, even if it was dark," said the sheriff.

"Did, for an instant. The lad that got nipped seemed like a big boy; tall, stout chap I should say, but the way he sprinted after the gun went off, he sure is agile."

"Did you hear them at the hangar?" Roberta asked.

"No. Fact is, we were in bed and my wife asked me to open our window a bit wider. These spring nights are warming considerable. I just got the window up when the shot came. The lad at the door surely had a vocabulary! Then the second shot ripped about and the fat fellow squealed."

"It was fortunate that you happened to be in the neighborhood, Mr. Howard," said Mrs. Langwell.

"I was cutting across lots for home when I heard the shots. I'd been at the town hall where we had a hot session over some concessions and taxes. Just got through and I was so tired I was for getting home by the shortest route, even if it took me through other people's property," explained the sheriff.

"We are very much—" Just then a motorcycle sputtered up to the house and its rider flung himself off vigorously. Before he could knock, Mr. Langwell was at the door and threw it open.

"Hello, I say, I happened to be riding near here, sort of meandering along not making much noise and I passed a big car parked back of those elm trees. Thought it was a spooning party, so came along minding my own business, then I heard shots and almost at the same time the motor of the limousine was started. I put on the brakes just in time to keep from hitting a man who was running toward the road, and he hopped into the car, another fellow right after him."

"Did you turn round and chase them?" Roberta asked eagerly.

"Yes, Miss, I did, but they opened her up and went 'hell bent for election,' I beg your pardon. And pretty soon I couldn't see anything but the dust they made, and there was plenty of that." He fumbled in the pocket of his jacket.

"Get the number?" the sheriff snapped.

"Bet your socks," the boy grinned. "Here she is."

"Good piece of work." Mr. Howard took the scrap of paper upon which the license number had been hastily scrawled.

"Wrote it down quick so I wouldn't forget it. Anybody hurt?"

"Thank you, we are all right," Mrs. Langwell assured him. "Won't you have a cup of coffee, or something to eat?" The chap was about Harvey's age.

"Thanks just the same. I'll ooze along. You people will want to get back to bed. If you care to bump-the-bumps with me, sheriff, I'll give you a lift on this cycle."

"Thanks. I'll get home as fast as I can and start things humming on the telephone. Spread this number over the country through the broadcasting stations and find out who owns that car."

"Ought not to be hard finding the would-be thieves," the boy grinned.

"Looks as if it might be easy, thanks to your good sense."

"Say it with flowers," the lad chuckled. "Come along. As long as I live I may never get another chance to have a sheriff in the saddle behind me. How I wish a cop would try to stop me on this trip."

The pair went off amid the reports of the motorcycle, and then the neighbors, assured that the Langwells were unhurt and in no further danger, departed. Before she went to bed Roberta took another look at the old barn-hangar where Nike and the Falcon were still resting securely. With a sigh of relief she glanced toward the sky, which was mighty dark, but she caught the faint outline of the moon shining through as if she had decided to lighten things up a bit in the vicinity of the beloved airplane and its owner. In spite of the excitement and terror, the girl was so weary that she dropped off to sleep at once and it was late when she awakened. To her amazement she heard voices in the vicinity of the hangar, but when she hopped out of bed, she saw it was her Dad there with the village electrician.

"Good morning, dear, I thought I heard you moving about."

"Morning, Mummy. What are they doing out there?"

"Your father decided to have a good alarm put on the door so that the next unwelcome hand that tries to tamper with it will wake up the neighborhood," she explained.

"Dad's a dear," the girl answered.

"I've always thought so," her mother admitted.

"And you have known him a lot longer than I have," Roberta chuckled.

"How would you like some breakfast here—"

"Top hole, but I'm going to get into some clothes and come down and get it before you spoil me entirely," she laughed and gave her mother a resounding kiss. "Oh, isn't it great that there was no damage really done!"

"Simply great."

"Did Mr. Howard get any news of the robbers?"

"We haven't heard anything from him this morning, but your father plans to stop at his office on the way in to town."

While Roberta was eating her belated breakfast any number of neighbors came in to congratulate the family because its property was safe, and, those who did not know the facts, to get details of the attempted theft. Once the conversation was interrupted by the sudden and sharp clanging of a bell which made them all jump. But Mrs. Langwell glanced out of the window and saw the electrician waving his hand so she knew he was merely testing the alarm, and reassured the callers.

"Sounds louder than the fire bell," Roberta remarked, and they agreed that she was right and it would certainly wake everybody in the neighborhood if it went off at night.

After the guests had taken their departure the girl helped her mother and when the bell was finally installed, they went out to inspect the job. The alarm was set low on the wall, the wiring ran back through the thick planks, which had been bored so they were not exposed, and could not be either ripped out or cut without difficulty.

"Keep them set all of the time," the man explained, "and remember whenever you want to open the door to switch them off. I'm to put some more on the windows, so your plane will certainly be well protected and ought to be safe."

"That's what we want," Mrs. Langwell told him, then turned to her daughter. "That is our telephone, dear."

"I'll go and answer it," Roberta replied, and ran to the house as fast as she could. The bell was still ringing so she knew that the party had not been discouraged over the delay and given up getting in touch with the family. "Hello," she spoke into the phone.

"I wish to speak with Miss Langwell," came the reply, and although the voice sounded familiar, Roberta could not recognize it immediately.

"This is Miss Langwell," she said.

"Miss Roberta Langwell?"

"Yes."

"How do you do! This is Mrs. Pollzoff."

"Oh!" Roberta wasn't at all delighted at the announcement.

"Today I went early to the field; waited for you an unreasonable length of time, then found, upon inquiry, that you are no longer with the Lurtiss Airplane Company."

"Yes."

"I was sorry, of course. Well, I took the liberty of asking them for your address and communicating with you. I prefer you to one of the men for my pilot; also your little plane rides very comfortably. This morning is wasted, but the afternoon is still young. I should like to engage you to take me along the coast as usual. Can you meet me in, say, half an hour?"

"Well—" Roberta hesitated.

"You will be well paid. You have not connected, as yet, with another firm, or taken on a passenger?"

"No," Roberta had to admit. Just then her mother came hurrying in lest the call be from her husband. She glanced at her daughter and saw the look of doubt on the young face.

"What is it, dear?" she asked softly. Roberta put the instrument low and spoke softly.

"Mrs. Pollzoff wants me to take her up this afternoon."

"Perhaps you will feel more comfortable if you are flying," her mother suggested.

"You will meet me?" came the demand in her ear.

"All right," she agreed.

"In half an hour."

"Yes." She hung up the receiver and explained the call to her mother, but she said nothing about her uneasiness of the day before. The idea of getting an immediate assignment did make her feel less dispirited, and when she thought of the previous afternoon, she dismissed it promptly. "Probably all poppy-cock," she told herself.

"It will not be difficult flying and if you have been taking her up every day, she may want to engage you regularly," Mrs. Langwell remarked. "I know you will feel better satisfied, although I was beginning to hope I should have you to myself for a few days."

"Ever get tired of me, Mummy?"

"Of all the idiotic questions ever asked, that takes the grand prize!" Mrs. Langwell answered. "Can I help you?"

"Of course you can."

The getting ready did not take long, and exactly half an hour later, Nike lighted about a mile from the Flying Field where the girl Sky-Pilot found her passenger had just arrived. The woman came in a taxicab, nodded a greeting, paid the driver, then came briskly to the waiting plane. Her throat was wrapped in a scarf.

"I am glad that you could come," she said, but the words were stilted, not especially cordial, and again that inexplicable feeling of uneasiness swept over Roberta.

"It was good of you to think of me," she responded, although she very much wanted to open the throttle and go sailing off, leaving her passenger to seek another pilot to take her on her mysterious mission. However, she suppressed the desire and opened the door of the cockpit instead. Mrs. Pollzoff took her place and quickly adjusted herself, but it wasn't until Nike had them high in the air a few moments later that Roberta noticed the woman had a bit of gauze and a long strip of courtplaster on her lower jaw. They were sailing over the eastern corner of the Lurtiss Field and a pang of sadness made Roberta blink hard as she glanced down at the familiar scene.

There near the end was the long hangar with the pilots' quarters close by. The middle of the ground was marked off for landing, runways, lights and signals. Further along, to one side were the special houses for special planes; Nike used to occupy one of them, and beyond them was the huge factory building, nearly all glass, with the executive and other offices facing the road. If she closed her eyes for a moment, Roberta could picture every inch of the whole plant. Here and there were animated-looking objects which she knew were men or women workers; the bus and one of the company's cars were racing along like a couple of toys. Resolutely she turned her face away and applied herself with determination to the task at hand. Once she noticed that Mrs. Pollzoff was looking at her in the mirror, but she smiled behind her goggles. She wasn't going to let her passenger know how she felt about being separated from her former work, its varied interests, and happy companionships.

"Straight west," Mrs. Pollzoff directed with apparent indifference.

They had been flying but a short time when Roberta became conscious that a second plane had risen from the take-off grounds she knew so well, and although she longed to look back, or give her wings the three-waggle-signal, she held Nike at a respectful angle. The machine came racing swiftly and once she caught a glimpse of it as it flashed into her mirror. The pilot was zooming higher than Nike and although the distance was too great for her to tell who was flying it did look like Larry's plane. The sight of it gave her another pang of loneliness, then, for companionship's sake, she glanced at the woman beside her and again noticed the bit of white adhesive which protruded above the chinstrap of her helmet.

"Wonder what happened to her face," was her mental question, but the answer was doubtless any one of a dozen possibilities and she didn't waste time in surmises. Mrs. Pollzoff took up the speaking tube and Roberta attached the end so she could hear what was to be said.

"You have an exceptionally fine plane," Mrs. Pollzoff remarked.

"I think so," Roberta answered with a smile.

"Care to sell it?" The girl was so astonished that she gasped.

"No, indeed, I do not," she answered emphatically.

"I am anxious to purchase a good one, and am willing to pay well for this," the woman persisted.

"Not for sale at any price. I wouldn't part with it," was the positive answer, and Mrs. Pollzoff smiled.

"I should have known that you would rather part with an eye. Let us turn back—I am a little tired today."

"All right." Nike climbed and curved widely, and then Roberta noticed two planes in the air, one coming up from the south, and the other rushing north. They were both going at a swift speed and it struck the girl pilot that this was the first time she had been out with Mrs. Pollzoff that planes had come anywhere near them. It also flashed through her mind that perhaps the presence of the flyers was the reason for her passenger's sudden weariness, but as far as she could tell the woman was not conscious of their presence in the air. Once or twice she glanced indifferently at the water, then, when they were soaring in fine style over Long Island, the field glasses were put in their case.

"Where shall I take you?" Roberta asked.

"To the Huntington depot, or as near as you can."

"It's some distance from the railroad."

"I can get a lift."

Presently they were gliding to earth, but before she alighted Mrs. Pollzoff turned again to her pilot. "You do not care to change your mind about selling your plane?"

"Nike isn't for sale!"

"Very well. I have some work, observation work which will take me greater distances. It is something in which my husband was interested, a theory of his; he left copious notes, but they are unfinished and I am occupying myself in trying to complete his work." Her voice sounded weary and Roberta suddenly felt sorry for her.

"It is fine that you can carry on for him," she said.

"I suppose so. The question is, can you accompany me on a more or less erratic course for about ten days or two weeks? Your plane is especially adapted for my purpose; it is comfortable and durable. I have no license, so could not fly it even if I purchased it, so, if I can hire you both, that will answer nicely."

"Well, I—"

"You will be well paid—"

"I wasn't thinking of the money," Roberta said hastily. "I'll have to talk it over with Dad and Mother. What shall I tell them I am expected to do?"

"Nothing more than you have been doing," she answered with a smile. "I'll call your home tomorrow evening and you can give me your answer."

CHAPTER IV
A STARTLING DISCOVERY

Flying home at a good speed Roberta considered the offer she had just received and tried to decide whether or not she cared to accept it. Today was the first time since they had started the trips together that her passenger had showed any signs of being especially companionable and her sadness had instantly aroused the young pilot's sympathy, but she was still not attracted by the woman; in fact she found an indefinable something which she positively disliked. The girl realized that Mrs. Pollzoff's attention was entirely absorbed with her own project and efforts to carry on her husband's work; also that while flying her own mind must be fully occupied with her job; but the taciturnity of the woman seemed more than concentration on her affairs, whatever they were. There was something hard in her expression and her jaw set more like an over-bearing man's than a woman's.

Thinking of the jaw the girl wondered about the strip of plaster which evidently protected some wound, and she tried to figure what it might be. This persistence of her mind in going back to the injured feature made Roberta impatient with herself; it seemed to her that she was trying to find out something which was both unimportant and none of her business. Anyone might get a bump, a bruise, a cut, or an insect bite on her face, and keeping it covered was nothing more than ordinary common sense, especially when her face might be exposed to the force of the wind while they were flying.

Glancing at her watch she calculated that she would reach home about the same time her father did and they could talk the matter over, but when she thought of her uneasiness regarding her prospective employer she realized that she really had nothing tangible to tell him. There wasn't a thing that Mrs. Pollzoff had said or done which could be used as an excuse for refusing the offer. By that time Nike was near their village, so Roberta throttled the engine and glided down close to the hangar entrance, which was open to admit her, for Mrs. Langwell had heard the familiar roar in the heavens, shut off the alarm and shoved the entrance wide.

"Thanks, Mummy," Roberta called as she rode past. Presently she was out of the cock-pit, but before the two reached the veranda, Mr. Langwell's car came rolling up the drive.

"Hello, children," he shouted cheerfully. The auto was quickly put in its own section of the old barn and he joined them.

"Hear anything from the sheriff?" Roberta inquired first thing.

"Not much. The license of the car is registered under the name of Pollzoff, a woman, but that is as much as I got—"

"Pollzoff?" Roberta exclaimed in amazement, then again into her mind leaped the memory of that scar on her cheek.

"Yes. Howard said he'd drop in this evening and give us further details, if there are any."

"Why, Dad, that's the name of the woman I was taking along the coast. I took her again this afternoon."

"You did!"

"And today she had a piece of tape on her chin, as if it had been hurt in some way."

"Humph. Well, my dear, it seems hardly possible that the woman would come herself and try to take your plane."

"Do you think Dad hit her with some of that shot?" Mrs. Langwell asked quickly.

"I don't know, Mummy. That piece of tape has been on my mind all afternoon; I couldn't keep from wondering about it," Roberta answered, then went on, "She wants me to take her on a trip."

"Well, we'll certainly look into the lady's reputation before you do anything of that kind," Dad declared positively. "Suppose we take a run down to Howard's office and talk it over with him—"

"Suppose you come in and eat your dinner before it is spoiled," Mrs. Langwell interrupted. "You can go later, or telephone him."

"Guess you're right," Dad grinned. "I'm hollow as a bass drum and there is no such desperate rush about the matter." The startling discovery formed the chief topic of conversation during the meal.

"The name is an unusual one but there may be others in the country," Mrs. Langwell remarked. "But it does seem odd that it should be her car and that she should have a wound of some kind on her face this morning."

"It's all circumstantial," Mr. Langwell added. "Did she usually come to the flying field in a taxi?"

"No, she came in her own car. I didn't think anything about the taxi today, but she might have used that because she was uncertain where we would land. We've come down in a different place every time I have taken her," Roberta explained.

"Still, I can't think that she herself would try to appropriate your plane. She has, as I understand it, limitless money," Dad said.

"That's what I heard at the office," Roberta admitted.

"How did the woman impress you?" Mrs. Langwell asked.

"Not very favorably," the girl admitted. "But when I tried to reason it out, I had nothing really to dislike her for."

"That sounds to me like Howard's car," said Dad as a machine came up the drive. He raised himself in his chair and looked out of the window. "It's the sheriff. We'll have a talk with him." Presently the officer was admitted but his expression was one of disappointment.

"We haven't accomplished a thing in discovering those thieves, Mr. Langwell," he began. "The machine belongs to a Mrs. Pollzoff, all right, and it was found in Delaware on a side road late this afternoon. Probably been abandoned."

"Oh."

"The owner isn't a bit of help, for she reported her car missing late yesterday afternoon. She said she had been doing some flying, then drove into town to keep an appointment in a beauty parlor. When she was fixed up and came out to go home, the limousine was gone. She reported it right away, and as I said before, it was discovered today."

"Oh. Did you see her?"

"No. There wasn't any use in doing that. Whoever had been driving was mighty careless for it was covered with mud from stem to stern. You hit one of the fellows, and I figure they went as fast and as far as they could, then stopped to get the wound dressed. The police are making inquiries among the doctors hereabout trying to find one who had a late call to attend to a split-open jaw. I'll meander along, I promised the wife I'd take her to the movies tonight. Sorry there isn't anything better to report."

"Thank you for coming in and telling us. After all, no one was hurt and the planes are safe," said Mrs. Langwell.

"That's right," Dad added. "And I've had a fine alarm system put on the hangar, so if anyone comes prowling around again, he will wake the world."

"Good thing. Well, good-bye." The sheriff drove off and the family returned to the unfinished meal. All of them were mighty sober.

"Just goes to show how perfectly damning circumstantial evidence can be, doesn't it? Here's a woman, one who knows flying, whose face has been injured in some way unknown, and whose car is seen parked near here for the robber's getaway. You know, if she hadn't reported the limousine missing things might have been very unpleasant for her," Dad remarked thoughtfully.

"And she is probably doing exactly what she says—just trying to carry on her husband's unfinished work. Don't you think it will be all right for me to tell her I'll take her on the trip, Dad? I feel sort of ashamed of myself for being so suspicious of everything."

"Guess it would, dear. Suppose I make a few judicial inquiries to be on the safe side. She isn't to call up before tomorrow evening, and by that time I can know a little about her," he replied.

"That's a good idea," Mrs. Langwell agreed, so it was left that way.

"How about taking my family to the movies?" Dad proposed, and they accepted without a dissenting vote.

The evening was spent delightfully, and the next afternoon Mr. Langwell called up from the city to inform his daughter that as far as it was possible to learn, Mrs. Pollzoff was above reproach. She had a great deal of money, a part of which she had made herself by first class business investments, and the rest she had secured when she sold her husband's fur business. She had a reputation for being quiet and conservative, considerate of her employees and active on several very worth-while philanthropic boards. So Roberta packed a bag for the trip and during the remainder of the time, attended to giving Nike a good inspection.

"Wish I could drop down on the field and give her to one of the mechanics to fix up," she said regretfully. She meant that there was not time to do it, not that she felt she couldn't ask for the accommodation, for she was positive that the courtesy would be extended to her cordially. She had nearly finished the task when her mother called, and when she went to answer the telephone, found it was Mrs. Pollzoff.

"I have called for your answer, Miss Langwell," came the rich voice.

"If you could see my suitcase and the way I have been working on the plane, you would know it," Roberta said as pleasantly as she possibly could.

"Then you will go."

"Very glad to," she replied.

"Meet me tomorrow at Elizabeth. I shall be there at eleven o'clock. Is that too early?"

"Not at all," Roberta replied. They talked a few moments longer about the meeting place.

"I presume you will fetch a warm coat."

"Oh, yes, I have it all ready. Thank you." She hung up the receiver and although she was trying hard to feel glad about the prospect before her, she wished heartily that she had said no, or that she could have said she had other work to do. "I'm a little idiot," she told herself, and then went back to the plane to finish getting it ready.

The next morning at a few minutes before eleven, Nike brought her out of a lower-sky near the New Jersey town and a few minutes later, Mrs. Pollzoff drove up in her own car. Roberta noticed that its fender had been bent, and when the woman alighted, she stopped a moment to speak to the chauffeur about having repairs made. He listened respectfully, then transferred her luggage to the waiting Nike, where he assisted in storing it safely.

While these final preparations were going on, Roberta heard a plane flying so low that she glanced up to see if the machine was coming down with its engine running, but she decided that the pilot must have had some difficulty in the take-off. He was climbing rather slowly, and she wondered if he was an inexperienced amateur in trouble or showing off to admiring friends who might be watching him.

"Is that all, Madame?" the chauffeur asked.

"Yes, thank you, that is all. We are quite properly packed, I think, Miss Langwell, but you had better make sure." Roberta glanced at the tiny baggage compartment, which was certainly well filled, and nodded. "Then we can start as soon as you are ready."

"I am ready now," Roberta told her. Mrs. Pollzoff took her place, adjusted straps and chute, nodded to the chauffeur, who was already back in the battered limousine, then glanced at the sky.

"Go south, toward Florida, about twelve miles out. The weather looks a little doubtful, we may as well have the cover over our heads," she said.

"All right." Roberta slid the top into place and made it secure, then assuring herself that she could start without cutting anyone in two with the propeller, she opened the throttle. The engine roared, Nike moved forward swiftly, lifted thirty feet further along, then rose majestically into the air. They zoomed, circled in wide loops, ascending in spirals, and at five thousand feet, leveled off. Roberta set the plane's nose toward the Atlantic, for she knew that her passenger preferred to travel above the water rather than the land. Ten minutes later the shore line was almost completely hidden by the haze which was lowering over the coast. Straight east they flew, only once seeing another plane. It was a small one which came alongside in a friendly fashion, but the distance was too great for the girl to see who was at the controls. Nike was twenty miles out when Mrs. Pollzoff indicated that she wanted to turn south, and in a moment that was accomplished. The sky did not look as threatening as it had from the shore and Roberta hoped that if a storm was brewing, she was going to get away from it.

They had been traveling about an hour when Mrs. Pollzoff got a book out and opened it, preparing to read. Roberta switched the light on so she could see better, and the woman glanced at the control board, seemed to make a mental calculation of the figures and dials, nodded, and then bent again over her reading. It wasn't anything more suspicious than a mystery story and for the next half hour the woman did not lift her head again. She seemed perfectly indifferent to everything but the story. The little plane that had followed them out had fallen behind and lower, and the girl Sky-pilot judged that its speed was not very great. She wished it would come alongside because it is always rather jolly riding with another machine in the air. In less than an hour it had been left far behind.

Early in the evening Nike glided down at Charleston, W. Virginia, where Mrs. Pollzoff had arranged for refueling and accommodations for the night at a small hostelry near the flying field. They took a cab to the hotel, which was an interesting old place, with a long low-ceilinged dining room. The apartment was a comfortable one with three rooms and bath and while they were refreshing themselves the woman broke the silence.

"As a companionable person I am not a great success, Miss Langwell. Tonight I am a bit fatigued and I think I shall have dinner sent up, but if you have never been in this place and are not too tired, I am sure that you will enjoy the atmosphere of downstairs. This house used to be patronized by members of Virginia's old families, and a few still cling to it; you may find it interesting."

"Thank you, I believe I shall, but I will be up early. Are you planning to leave in the morning?" Roberta asked.

"I do not know. It depends upon how I feel and what the weather looks like. I shall retire as soon as I have finished dinner," Mrs. Pollzoff answered. With her helmet off the gauze and tape completely covered the wound on her chin, and when she thought of her former suspicions, the girl Sky-pilot wanted to apologize for her stupid idea that her employer could possibly have been in any way connected with the attempted theft of Nike. She hurried with her dressing, and before she was ready, the waiter appeared with the tray.

"Anything I can do?" Roberta asked.

"Not a thing, thank you. Take your key, for I shall probably be asleep by the time you return."

"I have it. Good night."

"Good night."

Roberta made her way along the winding hall of the old house and decided that the house was one of those which had been built a good many years ago with later wings and additions. Twice she had to step down a couple of steps, and once around a sharp corner she had to go up three. However, she had no difficulty in getting to the main floor, which was cheery with old fashioned chandeliers that had yards of long crystals dangling so that the light sparkled through them, and the slightest breeze, or current of air passing set them tinkling merrily. Presently she was in the dining room and a very courteous old colored man, who looked as if he had stepped out of a picture of an ancient plantation home before the Civil war, showed her to a table from which she got an excellent view of the whole room.

Most of the tables were occupied, for it was late, but a few others came in when she was eating her first course. She noticed a party of young people, three men and two girls, who looked as if they were bound for a party of some kind, and when they were seated they made the place ring with their fun. They were rather a contrast from the other diners, but they were not boisterous nor ill-bred with their jollification.

"Pardon me, isn't this Miss Langwell!" It was a delightful Southern drawl and Roberta looked up into the eyes of Mr.

Powell, a young man who had taken the flying course under Mr. Wallace at Lurtiss Field, and whom she had helped pass his exams.

"Mr. Powell, how do you do?"

"Fine, Miss Langwell, and I am mighty glad to see you in our midst. I told my friends that I am going to ask you to join us; you look as if you are alone," Mr. Powell announced cheerfully. "Don't turn me down, for you can see we are desperately in need of another girl; especially since the two you see are my sisters." Roberta glanced at the other table and saw one of the girls coming toward her.

"How do you do, Miss Langwell," she greeted. "How delightful meeting you here. My brother has spoken of you often; I believe you taught him colors when he was taking his course in aviation. Please join us; we will be very pleased to have you."

"This is Helen, Miss Langwell. I am sure you cannot refuse her; no one ever does," the young man insisted, so Roberta accepted the cordial invitation and soon was one of the party. She was also introduced to Evelyn Powell and their cousins, Alton Manwell and Edward Crawford. There was no lack of sincerity and cordiality in their acceptance of the stranger, and as they were every one of them interested in aviation, they had no end of things to talk about.

"We are going to an amateur show and you must come along," Miss Powell informed the guest.

"We were to have another girl with us, but she had to break her engagement, so her ticket will not be wasted, and we shall have the pleasure of your company," Mr. Crawford added.

"It's rather a queer performance. You may be bored to death. Confirmed bachelor, Mark Anthony by name, but no relation to the ancient Cleo. He has a wonderful house, full of everything from every place in the world, and every once in a while he gives parties," Evelyn chatted.

"I didn't bring anything very party-like to wear," Roberta started to object, but they paid no attention to that.

"You look stunning and Helen has an extra scarf in the car. It will make you look more like a million dollars than you do," insisted Evelyn, so the matter was settled.

Roberta had been penned up in a cock-pit the greater part of the day, and a bit of fun was more than welcome. When the dinner was finished, the six of them were driven to the home of the confirmed bachelor and before his house they saw dozens of other cars lined up on both sides of the drive. They were led up the wide marble stairway, into a huge reception hall, where Roberta caught a glimpse of a very tall man who looked marvelously well in his evening clothes and was evidently the host. He was greeting the new arrivals pleasantly, and near him, facing the door they were entering, was an elegantly dressed woman, who glanced their way but was immediately shut off from Roberta's vision. But the one glance startled Roberta. It was Mrs. Pollzoff.

"She must have felt better after she finished dinner," Roberta remarked to herself, but when she reached her host's side, there was no sign of her employer, but she did not think anything of that, for the rooms were crowded.

CHAPTER V
A QUEER MYSTERY

When the performance was over and the guests were exclaiming about the charming entertainment they had seen, thanking Mr. Anthony for giving them such a delightful evening, and later taking their departure, Roberta glanced about for Mrs. Pollzoff, but did not see her. During the entertainment the rooms had been darkened except about the stage, so the girl Sky-pilot thought nothing of missing her employer then, but when the whole place was brilliantly lighted and the assembly moving somewhat like a narrow reception line, it seemed odd that the woman was nowhere in sight. With Miss Powell and her party, Roberta also thanked her host.

"I am very happy if my efforts have given such a charming stranger in our city an hour's pleasure," Mr. Anthony told her, speaking as if she were the only person in the room and had his undivided attention. Just then others came up, so she passed on with an impression that the gentleman, being a true Southerner, could make himself very agreeable.

"Anthony should be in the Diplomatic service," young Powell remarked when they were all in the car again.

"He always gives one a feeling that his only interest in life is to serve one," Helen added. "I am so glad that you could come with us, Miss Langwell. If you are going to be in

Charleston tomorrow, I shall be delighted to take you about a bit."

"That is something I will not know until tomorrow," Roberta told her. "You have been most kind. I should have had rather a dull evening had I not met you."

"Here we are at your hotel. Hope you can stay over," Powell said as he helped her out. She bade the others good night, thanked them again, then the young aviator saw her safely to the elevator. "I'll be on hand to help entertain you if you do not fly away."

Up in her own room, when Roberta switched on the light she noticed that the door between the two bedrooms was closed. She listened for a sound of anyone moving about, but the place was as still as if it was deserted. Before retiring, there was a note to be written to the family at home, and in it she told of the lovely old hotel with its aristocratic guests, the meeting with Powell and his sisters, the trip to Mr. Anthony's, and the fact that Mrs. Pollzoff was also there. Finally, adding no end of love for them all, she sealed the envelope, then went down the hall to the mail chute. When she returned there was still no sound from the other room and as she undressed, she tried to figure out why the woman had not nodded to her, and why she had disappeared like the foam on a ginger ale.

"Here I am imagining things about her again," she scolded mentally. "She probably knows Mr. Anthony and he persuaded her to come for a little while, then she went home and is now in bed asleep."

With this very logical conclusion she got into her own bed, switched off the light and immediately fell asleep, but she spent the night dreaming of vain efforts to fly away from Mrs. Pollzoff and the charming Mr. Anthony, who kept bobbing up, like a Jack-in-the-box, just when she was sure that she had left him behind, nor did she manage to evade the bachelor until she flew off over the North Pole. It was snowing, she thought, and she shivered as she brought the plane down, but instead of stopping, Nike dropped, and dropped and dropped until at last she struggled so hard to right it that she woke herself up. Morning had not put in an appearance, but the night had turned cooler and she had kicked off the covers, so with a sigh of relief that it was only a dream, she turned over and enjoyed a more restful sleep.

When she awakened she heard someone moving in the other room and guessed that Mrs. Pollzoff was already stirring. As the time had not been set for their departure, Roberta lost no time in dressing, and when she was finished, sure that her employer was up, she knocked at the door, but to her surprise received no answer. She tried again, without success, then someone tapped at her own door. It proved to be the maid who told her that word had been left that the woman was not to be disturbed, that she wished to sleep late. This was certainly puzzling, for the girl was positive that she had heard movements in the other room.

"Well, if she wants to take another snooze it's her own business. I wonder why in the dickens everything she does makes me uneasy?" she said to herself, and then prepared to go to breakfast. She took her key with her, and when she stepped out into the hall she was startled to see Mr. Anthony coming down the hall to Mrs. Pollzoff's door. If the man recognized her, he gave no sign of it, but glancing at the number, turned and went in the opposite direction as if he had made a mistake in the room. Again the feeling of uneasiness came over Roberta and she simply could not shake it off. At the desk downstairs she asked if her employer had left any word regarding when she intended to check out, and the clerk answered in the negative.

"Mrs. Pollzoff did not say when she is leaving, but she leases that apartment by the year," he explained obligingly.

Roberta went in to breakfast and when she had finished she was called to the telephone. It proved to be young Powell who wanted to know if she was staying in town but she couldn't give him any information. "I do not expect to leave right away," she said, and then explained the situation.

"Suppose Helen and I come up and in case you are not leaving soon we can bat around together?"

"That's mighty nice of you. I should be very glad to see you." It did not take the two Powells long to get there, and the three sought a quiet corner in the rambling old lobby.

"By the way, you have not said why you are here," Powell remarked.

"Why, Brother, what an impudent question," Helen protested.

"That's all right between aviators," he laughed.

"Of course it is," Roberta defended him quickly. "I really can not tell you why I came nor whither I go. I might say I came hither from thither and I am going hence; why do I not know."

"Sounds mysterious. What sort of bird is this Mrs. Pollzoff?" Powell inquired.

"She seems perfectly all right," was the answer.

"Why the seems—"

"Robert," Helen objected.

"I have a queer sort of feeling about her; I can't explain it. Last night she was at Mr. Anthony's but I only caught a glimpse of her, and this morning—" She broke off and flushed. "I have to admit that I am making a whole mountain range out of less than an ant hill, but the truth is, every simple thing she does seems mysterious. Guess I have been developing nerves."

"Tell me about it," Robert urged quietly. "If it's nerves, going over the facts will show them up in their true light and you'll feel better. We all get to a point where things do not seem right."

"Perhaps it would be a good idea," she admitted, then told him of her relations with Mrs. Pollzoff, leaving out nothing, not even the attempted theft of Nike.

"Humph," Powell grunted. "There really isn't a thing alarming in what you have told me, Roberta, but just the same, even though our reasons insist that everything is hunky—when you get a hunch as strong as the one you have, don't disregard it, that's my motto. I believe aviators have a sort of sixth sense that warns them, or tries to, and it's always a safe bet to pay strict attention. I've heard other flyers say the same thing, so, if I were you, I'd watch my step mighty carefully."

"Don't make her feel worse than she does," Helen urged.

"I'm not trying to; just want her to take every advantage of the faculty she has and not disregard a warning, even if it seems a foolish one. Here's our number and address; keep in touch with us and if anything comes up, get into communication with us right away." He took out his card and wrote the telephone number on it.

"We will all be happy to assist you in any way," Helen added.

"Thank you so much."

"Miss Langwell, Miss Langwell," called a page.

"I am Miss Langwell," Roberta told him.

"Mrs. Pollzoff would like you to go up," he told her.

"All right. I'll say so-long for now, and thank you so much."

"Hope we can see you again before you leave," Helen said, and just then they saw Mark Anthony strolling leisurely through the lobby.

"Humph," grunted Powell, "I never saw him here before."

"Isn't he an Old Family?" Roberta asked mischievously.

"No, he's a New Family; rotten with money, so he gets and does anything he wants to. Glad to have seen you, even for a little while."

Roberta took the card, then hurried to the elevator and presently came to her own room. The connecting door was open, so she went in immediately and found Mrs. Pollzoff in negligee, the wound on her chin covered with adhesive tape. A waiter had left a tray a few moments before and the woman was preparing to eat her breakfast.

"Did you have a good night?" she asked politely.

"Very pleasant," Roberta answered. "I met an old friend, Robert Powell, and his sisters at dinner and they took me to a theatrical at Mr. Anthony's home."

"Then you were not bored with Charleston. I do not care for the place and rarely go out. The people seem to me excessively stupid, and the city, most of it, antiquated. Did you have breakfast?"

"Yes, thank you."

"The maid said you had gone down, so I ordered only one. I had a wretched night, thought I should never get to sleep, but when I did I made up for it by not waking until fifteen minutes ago," Mrs. Pollzoff said and her statements startled the girl.

Roberta wondered if the woman was claiming that she had not left the room since they parted the evening before, but she refrained from saying anything more about the theatricals. She was absolutely convinced that it could have been no one else who was standing beside Mr. Anthony as he received his guests, and she was also convinced that her employer had been up that morning before she herself was awake. Why the woman should deliberately lie over anything so trivial made Roberta recall Powell's warning to watch her step, and, casting logic aside, she determined to pay heed to what he had said.

"I am sorry you did not have a more comfortable night," she replied, then added, "The page said you wanted me."

"Yes. I wanted to be sure that you had breakfasted and to tell you that we will leave here about one o'clock, so have your lunch before you go, and if you want to do any errands, you can," Mrs. Pollzoff said.

"Guess I haven't much in the way of errands but I'll tell them to have—"

"I have already notified them to have the plane in readiness."

"Then I shall not need to bother. I see there is a store near the hotel; I'll run up there and get some handkerchiefs. I came away without a good supply," Roberta told her, then, as the woman seemed to have nothing more to say, she returned to the lobby very uneasy in mind.

For less than two pins Roberta would have told her employer that she was returning home at once, but such an act appeared more foolhardy than cautious. It took only a few minutes to get the handkerchiefs she required, then she saw attractive cards of the city, and stationery. On the impulse of the moment she bought paper and envelope and wrote a hasty note to Robert Powell, telling him that she was leaving in a couple of hours, the place where Nike had been left, and expressing a wish that if he had his own plane and could come waggling his wings to her as they had in the days when they were both learning to fly she would feel easier. She added a word of thanks to his sister, then signed her name, but after that she put in the fact that Mrs. Pollzoff had said she was in her room all night—as if she had not been to Mr. Anthony's.

"I know I'm awfully silly, but at the next landing I am going to resign from the job.

"Sincerely yours,

Roberta Langwell."

"Can I get a messenger to deliver this?" she asked the woman who had been serving her.

"I'll take it, lady," a small boy offered, so at a nod from the woman she gave him a coin and made sure that he knew where to go. "Aw, that isn't far away," he said scornfully, and tucking it into his pocket, he raced off with the letter. As soon as he had gone, Roberta wished she had not been so silly as to tell Robert Powell such a trivial matter. After paying for her purchases she returned to the lobby where she sat at one of the desks, wrote a note and sent cards to the family. That finished, she ate her lunch in the dining room, but felt so uncomfortable that she didn't enjoy it at all.

Promptly at one o'clock they left the hotel in one of its own buses and drove quickly to the small flying field where they found Nike already wheeled out of the hangar. Although a mechanic was beside the plane, the girl Sky-Pilot took time to assure herself that everything was as it should be, while Mrs. Pollzoff took her place in the cock-pit.

"I went over everything, Miss," the mechanic told her.

"Thank you, I know you did, but where I learned to fly one of the things they stressed was to be positive yourself that things were all right. You certainly did a good job and you put in a full supply of gas."

"Those were orders," he told her. She climbed to her own place, and when at last all was as it should be, she nodded to him, and he gave them a start, not that he needed to, for Nike was a self starter in every way; perfectly capable of taking off without assistance. The chap stood watching the plane with keen admiration, and when she lifted, Roberta waved him a farewell.

Quickly they climbed to three thousand feet, then Mrs. Pollzoff signaled that it was high enough. She picked up the speaking tube and Roberta listened, for the woman never gave her directions until they were started.

"Turn in a half circle, then go straight northwest until I tell you to change the course or come down," she said. Nike promptly did the turn and then leveled off, her nose pointing the route indicated. Roberta was surprised, for they were going inland instead of over the water as usual. Glancing at her chart she reckoned that the course would take her across the United States into the southwestern part of Canada, provided they continued long enough. Mrs. Pollzoff sat watching the control board for a few minutes, then proceeded to produce another book and buried herself in its pages.

"I believe that her saying she is carrying on some work started by her husband is just so much bologna. We haven't done a blooming thing since we started—except fly—and she certainly isn't accomplishing anything while she's reading a mystery story. That's that. And I'm dropping out of the business at the next stop—that is more of that," was the girl's mental resolve, and she set her lips in a firm line to emphasize her resolution.

They had been in the air less than ten minutes, when suddenly, out of the sky to the right, and higher than Nike was flying, swept a shining new plane, its wings waggling furiously. Roberta's heart gave a great leap, and she responded, but not quite so vigorously as Powell. His plane swooped down across her path and as it flashed by she could see that he was not alone. Whoever was in the cock-pit with him waved a gloved hand, and Roberta replied to that also. Not changing her course by a hair, Nike roared steadily on, the other plane circled about her once, then with a final waggle, zoomed up, spiraled, and then turned back. The girl Sky-Pilot smiled as her friends disappeared, then she happened to look into the mirror and saw that Mrs. Pollzoff had been watching the performance with an interest which was none too kindly.

"Who are they?" she snapped.

"Robert Powell and his sister," Roberta told her. "The people I met last night." They were using the telephone.

"How do they happen to be here when we start?" For an instant Roberta was going to tell her the truth, that she had sent word she was leaving and Powell had come to see her off, but his warning to "watch her step" flashed through her mind.

"I do not know how they happen to be around," she answered, which was true enough. "Guess he saw the plane go up and came over to say goodbye in case it was Nike." There was a peculiarly hard look in Mrs. Pollzoff's eyes during the explanation, and she looked steadily at her pilot for several seconds, then dropped her eyes back to her book.

CHAPTER VI
KIDNAPED

As Roberta attended strictly to her business she became thoroughly convinced that her "hunch" regarding her employer was well worth heeding; that the woman's mission was not only mysterious and confusing, but that it was an enterprise with which she did not care to be associated a minute longer than that she could possibly help. Following the course set, going higher when the country beneath them demanded it, or lower as permitted, she thought things out carefully. Nike did not carry gas enough to take her back to Long Island, but she had money enough with her to drop down onto a landing field and purchase more; also she knew that even if she hadn't the cash she could give them a draft on her bank in New York if they were not willing to accept a check.

Carefully studying the chart, which she knew almost by heart anyway, she realized that the route they were following was, for the most part, well out of the usual air lines, but there were several places where she would fly parallel or across those laid out. Roberta thought of the towns and cities over which they would pass, calculated their location and which ones she would be near early in the evening, when the woman beside her would probably order a landing. They had been flying nearly three hours when Mrs. Pollzoff glanced up at the speedometer.

"I wish that you would go a little faster," she directed, so the Girl Sky-Pilot nodded and opened up a bit wider, but she did not put on full speed. They had been averaging eighty miles an hour, so she increased it to ninety-five, which meant that when conditions permitted she was doing more, and less when the air and country were not so favorable. Another hour passed and Roberta began to wonder when they were to come down, but Mrs. Pollzoff still seemed absorbed in her book, although Roberta was positive that she was not so intent as she was trying to pretend.

Glancing at the sky, Roberta saw, far ahead, a dark cloud rising in the west which looked as if it might cause them trouble in the course of a few hours, but she paid little attention to it for she figured they would have landed before the storm reached them, or they reached it. To get a better view of the world, she gradually increased her height a thousand feet. Roaring swiftly along she saw, far ahead of them, a large plane which looked like one which carried passengers, and another time, when her eyes rested a moment on the mirror, she saw a small plane behind them. This looked like an ordinary machine with one passenger—or perhaps no one but its pilot, and while she watched the tiny speck, it dropped lower and out of her range of vision.

Studying the chart again, without seeming to do more than observe the various controls the girl Sky-Pilot looked for the nearest flying field. In another hour they would be over Wisconsin, for the end of Lake Michigan was tossing beneath them, and on its rough surface raced a huge speed boat across the great body in exactly the same direction that Nike was flying a mile above. The water was thickly dotted with numerous boats, large and small, but this little one, which looked no bigger than a dark dot with a long foamy tail, attracted the girl's attention because of its speed. Nike soon left it behind, however. Glancing about the horizon, she saw that they were well away from the storm, but she anticipated bad weather for the following day. A bit later, listening to the radio reports, this calculation of hers was confirmed by the Bureau from Washington.

From time to time Mrs. Pollzoff glanced up, studied the dials, chart and the whole array, for even if she hadn't qualified for a license, and could not pilot a plane, it was not because she did not thoroughly understand every bit of flying. She just happened to be one of the persons whose knowledge on the subject was not sufficient to make her act wisely at all times in any emergency. Even though she never asked to carry a passenger, wanted nothing more than to fly herself, a plane in the air piloted by a man or woman who might behave erratically, was a menace to the world below. She might suddenly crash into a building, come down with a blazing machine in a dry forest and start a fire which would do countless dollars worth of damage, or she might drop on a gas tank and blow the whole vicinity to tooth-picks.

Suddenly, as Roberta visualized the chart she realized that it would not be very long, according to the course they were following and the speed they were going, before Nike crossed the border into Canada. She would be on foreign soil without the usual curtsy to the Dominion, also they were getting further and further away from Long Island and her own home. If she was not going to continue the trip, why not stop now? As a matter of fact, why had she come so far at all; why hadn't she dropped down a couple of hours ago and informed Mrs. Pollzoff that she was not going on, land that lady wherever she wanted to be landed, then go on east? Silently scolding herself for her stupidity, the girl decided that if Mrs. Pollzoff did not order a descent within the next few minutes, Nike would make a landing without it. As if she rather suspected something of what was going on in her companion's mind, Mrs. Pollzoff closed her book, looked about at the sun, which had almost set, then taking a package from under the seat, proceeded to open it. To Roberta's surprise it contained food; it seemed enough for several generous meals, including thermos bottles with hot and cold drinks.

"We will have something to eat in the air," the woman announced quite casually, but there was something deadly in her tone. However, Roberta had herself well in hand and she answered firmly.

"I am sorry, Mrs. Pollzoff, but I am going down," she answered.

"Why?" the woman asked quietly.

"We need gas for one thing—"

"Not yet," Mrs. Pollzoff interrupted.

"I have been at the controls steadily and I do not believe that it would be safe for me to continue much longer without a rest and a proper meal."

"You will find everything that you can possibly get in a proper meal anywhere," Mrs. Pollzoff told her coolly, and added, "And as for a rest, I'll relieve you."

"I cannot permit that," Roberta answered. "Without a license you could not fly and my plane is different from the usual ones; I would rather not have anyone who is not accustomed to it try to operate it."

"Well, have something to eat," Mrs. Pollzoff said wearily. "It is still quite light. When I was learning to fly I once saw three sunsets. I'd very much like to get at least one more view of the sun tonight. Zoom Nike up high so that we will have a magnificent view to remember when we go to sleep tonight."

"All right," Roberta agreed with great relief. She was glad there was no argument and she resolved that she would not tell her employer she could not go on until they were safely landed.

So that there was no danger of getting over into Canada, she spiraled as she climbed and decreased the plane's speed.

"Should you like milk, tea or coffee to drink?" Mrs. Pollzoff asked as she arranged the food, which certainly looked appetizing, especially since Roberta had eaten almost no lunch.

"Tea, if it has plenty of milk and not too strong."

"Sugar, how many lumps?"

"A small one, thank you." The drinks were poured into deep paper cups which were half-filled carefully to prevent spilling. Nike was leveled, her dials and controls set so that her pilot could relax a bit and enjoy the meal. It was not long before they saw the sun again in all its splendor, and watched a second setting, which was certainly well worth waiting for because the air was clear and the countless brilliant rays, were flung fan-like from the rim of the horizon.

"Cake or pie, or will you have another sandwich?" Mrs. Pollzoff asked a bit later.

"Cake, it sounds simpler to consume," Roberta laughed. One simply couldn't help feeling secure, riding like a part of the gorgeous spectacle, and the girl wondered if she hadn't been premature in her decision to abandon her employer.

"I'll fill your cup again."

"Only half," Roberta said hastily.

"Cannot measure it," Mrs. Pollzoff smiled and her pilot thought if she were only as pleasant all of the time they might go on forever.

"Thank you. I do feel better. Guess I did not realize how hungry I was," Roberta told her.

"Didn't you have anything to eat before you left the hotel?"

"Just a salad, but I wasn't hungry then. This has tasted very good, every bit of it."

"Sure you have had enough?"

"Yes, thank you."

"You still have a tank of gas, haven't you?" Mrs. Pollzoff consulted the indicator to see how much was in the plane.

"Yes, but I believe we had better get down soon because we are getting away from towns and even farms. We do not want to be stranded in the open all night," Roberta consulted the chart.

"Very true. Have you done any night flying?"

"Oh yes, but not any oftener than I could help. Of course there are a great many guides and riding under the stars is mighty attractive but one never can tell what might happen; storms come up suddenly, and mountains have a disconcerting habit of bobbing in front of a plane when it is least desirable." They talked through the telephone and finally Roberta decided upon the best place for their landing, turned sharply off the course toward the southeast.

"Why do you go back?" Mrs. Pollzoff asked her.

"We will get better landing accommodations; at least, I know the field and I am sure of it," the girl answered.

"All right, one should never interfere with the pilot, but if we go forward we will have less distance to travel tomorrow."

"We have put half the continent behind us since we started," Roberta reminded her and the woman made no further objections.

They flew on for a quarter of an hour, then suddenly Roberta had a sharp pain between her eyes and she blinked in bewilderment, but it went away again quickly so she decided that it wasn't anything to worry about. However, she increased her speed, for if she was going to be sick, she wanted to get on the ground as quickly as possible. But now there was no sign of the sun, all of its brilliant colors had faded to dull grey, which was rapidly growing darker, and although the girl searched the heavens, she did not see a single star blinking back at her. Far in the distance she caught the faint flicker of a light which she was sure was the landing field she sought and a glance at the chart verified her calculation. Setting her course, she headed Nike in as straight a line as possible and decreased the speed, banked in preparation for the glide when she was near enough.

Then again came that stabbing pain, but this time it was in her head.

Brushing her hand over her forehead and opening the strap of her helmet she felt better again and she hoped hard that her companion would not notice that anything was wrong. Mrs. Pollzoff might go into a panic if she discovered her pilot was ill and perhaps do something in her excitement which would bring them all down in a smash. On they flew, the lights getting nearer and nearer; and bigger and bigger, then, suddenly, they began to dance into a long line which Roberta knew was an optical illusion. Glancing forward she decided that she could begin the descent, but when she reached toward the control-board, it seemed to get further and further away from her. Finally she managed to close the switch and forcing herself with every ounce of strength and courage she possessed, she struggled to make the field without a smash-up.

But, to the girl's amazement, she felt rather than saw, that Nike instead of starting toward the earth, began to climb steadily, moving in a wide circle; she could tell that by the wind in her face, then the plane rose more swiftly, thundering upward at top speed. Frantically the pilot endeavored to find the proper switches, but it was so dark that even in the lighted cock-pit she could not see the board nor its indicators, except in a blurred sort of way.

"Are you all right, Miss Langwell?" It was Mrs. Pollzoff's voice speaking through the tube.

"I am trying to go down, to make a landing—I'm—"

"You are trying to, but you are climbing and you are going to keep on climbing—"

"W-what—what do you m-mean—" Roberta tried desperately to gather her wandering faculties.

"Simply that you are obeying orders!"

"We can't f-fly at night," Roberta protested, then a feeling of horror swept over her, for suddenly she understood. Something she had eaten was paralyzing her faculties, making her helpless there in Nike, flying swiftly a mile above the ground and far from the landing field where she knew she had friends.

"Whether we can or not, we are going to." The woman forced her back in her seat and took over the management of the controls. "You will learn before you are much older not to have your aviator friends watching us when we take-off—"

"I didn't h-h—" But her voice trailed off, her head wobbled forward on her chest, and if Nike had started a nose dive that moment, her pilot could have done nothing to prevent her tearing straight to the ground and digging a ten-foot hole for herself in the ground. The girl, for a couple of moments was partly conscious, but that too left her quickly and she was completely out of the picture, at the mercy of the mysterious Mrs. Pollzoff, if she had any mercy, which was very doubtful.

Mrs. Pollzoff glanced with eyes that blazed hatefully at her unconscious companion, then, as she had to attend to several things immediately she first reset the course of the plane and when it was back in the route it had been pursuing when Roberta announced her determination to land for the night, then, as managing the machine from any other seat than the pilot's was an awkward one she loosened the girl's safety-strap and her own. Keeping an alert eye on the indicators she quickly made the transfer, and over her features came a look of keen satisfaction.

"You will taunt me that I could not get a license, and that only you can operate your precious Nike! Well, I'm going to operate it now and if it flies us both to death, you have it coming to you; you little fool." She laughed harshly, and into the dark eyes, which had worn nothing but boredom and indifference for so long, flashed insane fury. "For next to nothing, I'd dump you out of the cock-pit, you silly girl!"

For a moment she looked at Roberta as if determined to do just that, but finally she curbed herself, drew her companion's safety-belt tighter, and ran her fingers around it mechanically, for she had been thoroughly drilled in every phase of the work she longed with her whole soul to follow the rest of her life. Finding that as it should be, she saw to the chute and its rip-ring; assuring herself that in changing their places she had put nothing out of adjustment. Again she gave her attention to the plane, which was behaving perfectly, and as her fingers touched the controls her whole body tingled, as if the digits were lingering over some current which instantly filled her with life and animation.

Assured that all was as it should be she took a short strap from the food container and wrapping that twice about her victim's feet, buckled it on the side where she could see that it was not worked open; nor that it could be without the aid of fingers. Roberta had taken off her long gauntlet gloves while she ate and drank, so Mrs. Pollzoff slipped them back onto her hands. Then with a second strap she secured the girl's arms to her sides, but again the air-mindedness in her forced her to place the left one, which was nearest to her, close to the life saving rip-ring.

"Now, now," she laughed shrilly, and if Nike had been making less noise the sound might have startled the people beneath them, for it was so harsh and bitter that it was uncanny.

By that time the gas indicator showed that the plane required replenishing, so she poured in the reserve tank, calculated how long it would last her, did some mental figuring, then increased the speed until it was going at a dangerous rate. She had not done enough flying so that she was any too familiar with the surface of the country, so she zoomed high to avoid mountains. Her next act was to shut off the engine to listen for other planes whose pilots might be following her. As Nike glided to earth the woman heard two of them. One seemed to be far behind her; it might have come up when Roberta failed to land on the flying field. The other was directly south, apparently coming straight across her course.

92

CHAPTER VII
A PRISONER

Having ascertained that there were two planes in the air, Mrs. Pollzoff opened her throttle again, turned the machine as if she were returning to the field and glanced at the indicator to be sure that her nose and tail lights were on. Looking toward the other machines she mentally calculated their course and watched the one which was coming to the south of her. She noted with a scowl that when she came around it swerved off its route considerably, but the second pilot exhibited his lack of interest in her movements by rushing steadily forward, zooming to be well out of her way, and passing on toward the Canadian border.

"If you are following me I shall give you a good run for your money," the woman snapped furiously.

She lifted Nike's nose, climbed gradually to seven thousand feet, leveled off, then proceeded at an even keel, racing at the machine's top speed; then she started to descend, going more and more slowly, until the altimeter registered two thousand feet. At that level she shut off her engine a moment to listen, glanced at the chart, and then convinced that the larger plane was determined to keep tabs on her, she shut off the lights, and risked a smash-up by gliding to a thousand feet. She could see the larger plane high and in back of her, the roar of its engine sufficient to drown that of Nike; then she opened the throttle, keeping the head and tail lights out, throwing a cover over the dim light in the cock-pit, and began to climb slowly.

Nike rushed swiftly forward at its highest speed, lifting gradually and Mrs. Pollzoff kept her eyes on the covered control-board, shielding it so that the glow could not be seen by anyone in the air. Twice she glanced over her shoulder and through the blackness of the starless heavens could see the other plane moving more swiftly now toward the spot where its pilot must have calculated that she had made her landing. It was descending gradually and with a chuckle of satisfaction over the scheme she had planned to shake off possible pursuers, she lifted Nike's nose again and climbed more steeply. At ten thousand feet she came around in a wide sweep then reset her course for the northwest which they had been following since the take-off.

Occasionally she looked at the unconscious girl beside her, and once, when she saw by the clock how long it had been since Roberta passed beyond the realm of consciousness, she pressed her finger over the girl's wrist. In a moment she ascertained that the pulse was beating, although very slowly, then she drew up the gauntlet and unhooked the throat band of the coat.

"If you die, I don't give a care, but I'd rather you wouldn't, for I'm going to take a lot of the conceit out of you and your friends before I get through with you. But die if you want to, for I'll drop you overboard into one of the lakes. This part of the world is full of them and you'll go down so far they will never be able to tell that you didn't do it naturally. I'll see to that." She spoke as if she expected to be heard and understood, but Nike had hit a mighty rough place in the air and for the next five minutes demanded every bit of her attention.

Making a careful survey of the heavens and the world beneath her, she bared her teeth and grinned maliciously, because there wasn't a sign of another plane. She calculated that by the time the second pilot had shut off his engine to descend, if he did, Nike was too far on its way for them to hear its engine, so would be lost to them for good.

"And they won't pick me up again," she declared with satisfaction, but although she felt confident that she was safe from pursuit, she made it her business to be alert every moment.

The fact that the night was dark and there were no stars, helped her, for the instant a plane's light flashed into the sky she would be able to see it easily. By that time a stiff wind was blowing. It shrieked dismally through the struts and braces, and Nike plugged on and on with a wail of protest. One thing she watched with the greatest care was the engine, for she did not know how it would stand up on an endurance flight. But it was hitting steadily, behaving quite as if it had not traveled for hours and seemed perfectly capable of going on indefinitely.

They had crossed the border and were well into Canada when a slight movement on the part of her prisoner warned her that the girl was regaining consciousness. She glanced at the white face, saw the head move slightly, the lips part, but the movement ceased after a minute, and Roberta sank back into a state of unconsciousness. With so many things to observe, Mrs. Pollzoff grew less cautious and folded the cover she had spread over the cock-pit lights, but she dimmed everything except those she actually needed to read the dials in front of her. The wind was shrieking now, so she tried to set a course which would keep her out of the storm which she knew as surely rising, and continued the flight without showing a light.

According to the chart they were rushing over a mountainous section and here she zoomed high, lest they meet an obstruction. Her experience with altimeters had not included the latest model on Nike so she was fearful lest the instrument fail to warn her in time to avoid collision with the immovable face of a rocky cliff. Then examining the chart, she swerved sharply out of her course and suddenly, from far ahead she saw another plane circling in wide sweeps. It carried four lights, two blue, one red and the other green.

The sight of this airman gave Mrs. Pollzoff no terrors, for she blinked one of her lights for a moment, then switched it out again. This she repeated twice and flew steadily on until five minutes later the two machines were flying side by side, the other plane, which was larger, slightly above Nike.

In the meantime Roberta had returned to consciousness and was fully aware of what was going on about her. The drug she had been given had caused a sort of paralysis but her mind had cleared several minutes before she stirred. The first thing she knew was the fact that Mrs. Pollzoff's fingers were pressed against her wrist but at that time she was utterly unable to move so much as an eyelash, so she remained as if still completely under the influence of the dope which had been given to her in something she ate. Her head ached furiously, and it seemed as if pins and needles were pricking her whole body.

Slowly the sensation, except the headache, faded, and she was able to think. She tried to remember of what Mrs. Pollzoff had accused her when the drug began to take effect, but she couldn't remember. By the feel of the plane, the girl Sky-Pilot was able to tell something of how they were flying and she tried to form a plan of escape. As her body recovered she had ventured to move, and in this way had ascertained that she was strapped tightly and was helpless in the passenger seat. The effort to move had been excruciating and when she relaxed again it was as much exhaustion as design.

By the shrill whistle through the struts Roberta knew that they were flying against a high wind, and as Nike bucked forward, her engine roaring, and every part of her wailing a protest, she was sure that Mrs. Pollzoff must be fully occupied with the task of keeping the plane balanced. There were times when it fairly jumped, others when it half twisted, and more when the wings dipped under the force of the on-rushing storm, and creaked as if they were being ripped off the fuselage.

Cautiously the girl lifted one eyelid and verified her calculations for Mrs. Pollzoff was leaning far forward in the seat, battling with every ounce of strength and knowledge she possessed. There was almost no light in the cock-pit and Roberta wondered if they were flying without head and tail lights. She wished she could get a glimpse of the control board. What she wanted to see most was the clock, which would tell her how long she had been unconscious. She reasoned that it was not likely they had landed anywhere; for a trussed girl would certainly arouse suspicion and immediate demands for an explanation. If the fact that she was bound went unobserved, still it would be noticed that she was either asleep or ill; someone would be sure to investigate.

If they had not landed, and had traveled any length of time at the speed they were going, the gas supply must be nearly exhausted. Venturing to open her eyes wide and look at the sky all she could see was pitch darkness so that did not help her discover how long she had been unconscious, but she had a positive hunch that it had been some hours. If this was right they would be compelled to land soon to replenish the fuel supply.

Mrs. Pollzoff had drawn on her gauntlets, but she hadn't made a very smooth job of it. There was a rip in the lining of the right one and Roberta's finger had gone in the wrong way. It was the hand nearest the outside of the cock-pit, so she risked moving it slightly, then she wondered if she couldn't do something after all to leave a clue as to which way she went. All of her flying clothes were marked with a stamp in indelible ink with her full name. This included the inside of her gauntlet cuffs.

Roberta's heart hammered hopefully as she stealthily wriggled her fingers, pressing them tightly to her side and moving her arm back. She couldn't do this more than half an inch, but repeating the performance patiently and with the utmost caution she finally succeeded in getting her hand well out. Then, waiting a moment, the next time Nike gave a bump, she flipped the glove as high as she could, and with one half-opened eye, she rejoiced to see that the plane dropped sharply, the wind caught the thing as if it were a leaf and bore it off into the darkness. The girl knew that it would probably land miles from where it left her and she prayed that it would be found soon. She knew, also, that it would probably be some time before her absence or disappearance was noticed. Mrs. Langwell would have the letters from Charleston, and when no more arrived she would start an inquiry. Her dad would get in touch with Mr. Trowbridge or Mr. Wallace.

Even though she was no longer an employee of the Lurtiss Airplane Company, Roberta hadn't the slightest doubt that the firm, its entire force if necessary, would be put out to search for her. She could hear Phil Fisher's wrathful explosions, and see Larry marching out after the best machine, climbing grimly into its cock-pit and roaring furiously off in pursuit. Thinking of the loyalty of every one of them she wondered if Mrs. Pollzoff realized it and hoped hard that the woman didn't. Of course everyone knew perfectly well that any pilot, man or woman, who was lost immediately became the focus of the world's attention until the plane appeared or the wreck was discovered; but everyone could not appreciate the perfect camaraderie which existed in the firm's organization; especially among the flyers. If it was rumored that Miss Langwell was missing nothing would be left undone to locate her.

Roberta had no doubt that Mrs. Pollzoff would take every possible precaution, and now the girl thought of the possibility of escaping when they came down for fuel. She tried again to catch a glimpse of the control board but that was hopeless, so she gave it up. It was a strain to remain in the same position but she forced herself to do it for she was positive that the instant her captor realized that she had come to her senses, she would take further precautions to see that there was no opportunity for her to get away.

Suddenly, on the wind which came to her, she smelled a strong tang of salt water; enough so that she decided they were nearing one of the coasts and that the storm was coming from there. The air was only intermittently salty so she guessed they were still some distance away from the ocean, whichever one it was. Then through the darkness and to her right, she saw a plane flying high and carrying four lights. Almost at once the lights on Nike were flashed, then Roberta was sure that they had been traveling without them. Evidently the woman had been afraid of some one's following after her. Now the course was changed sharply and presently Nike was racing to the left of a plane about twice as large as her own.

Although Roberta wanted to see what this was all about she dared not move, for she was sure that the other machine carried no friend of hers. Peeping cautiously she saw the machine zoom up sharply, they seemed to be going through some sort of maneuver. Mrs. Pollzoff had raised herself in the pilot's seat as far as the safety strap would permit, then in a moment the larger plane came around to the right. The girl Sky-Pilot promptly closed her eyes lest its pilot warn the woman that she was awake.

Twice the two planes circled, then the larger one rose sharply on Roberta's side, and a moment later she could see the underside of a monoplane; its huge floats looking like the bottoms of small flat boats. In another second something like a weight dropped into Roberta's lap and instantly Mrs. Pollzoff caught it up, so the girl decided that her captor must be receiving a message, or sending one by the other pilot, but the next instant something dragged across her knees and unable to contain herself any longer, she raised her lids, only to close them again quickly, for the woman was standing over her. At the moment her face was raised, but then she looked down.

What the girl Sky-Pilot saw made her gasp in astonishment and fear, for Mrs. Pollzoff was hauling in a long tube, which must mean that she was going to refuel from the air and not come down at all, at least until the supply was depleted. She might take on a full supply, as much as they had had when they left Charleston, and unless the woman went to sleep over the stick, she could keep going until the following day.

Sick with horror, Roberta tried to make her brain function properly, but it was filled with the wildest terrors and in spite of warm clothing, she felt as cold as if she were wearing summer clothing. In the day time, under the best of conditions, what the two planes were trying to do could be accomplished with skilled pilots at both controls, but in the middle of the night, with a woman at the receiving end of the tube who had been disqualified as a flyer, it was a desperately risky undertaking. Nike's nose might be jammed up into the other plane's underpinning or drop so low that the tube would be broken and the machine sprayed with the highly inflammable mixture. A dozen things could happen so quickly to make a smash-up inevitable. She wondered dully why Mrs. Pollzoff didn't take in new containers, which would be less dangerous, and when the girl recalled that the woman had been considered incompetent as a pilot, she was no longer surprised. Probably her examiners had realized that she was too foolhardy to trust with a license.

There were a number of slips, disconnections and reconnections during the performance, and it seemed to Roberta as if hours passed before the work was finally achieved and she felt the long tube with its heavy weight being dragged across her knees again and at last heard them thump and bump against the side of Nike while the other pilot hauled them up to his own machine. Then Mrs. Pollzoff resumed her seat and her appropriated task, but the girl felt her slip down as if weary from the strain. She opened her eyes a bit to see if the woman was able to do anything more and found that she was busy with the controls, and circling in a wide sweep, the second plane was soaring out of her way, the end of the tube extending behind. Then it disappeared from sight.

Again Roberta's nostrils were filled with that strong odor from the sea and Nike zoomed courageously forward, carrying with her every vestige of hope that she might help herself or get help when they were forced to land. There was not a chance in the world that they could come down for hours, unless the engine gave them trouble, and no one knew better than the girl Sky-Pilot that every inch of her plane's machinery was the best possible and that it would stand long hours of the hardest grilling without showing a sign of weakness. She wondered over and over why Mrs. Pollzoff had kidnaped her and tried to remember what the woman had said as she was losing consciousness, but her head ached with the effort. Then she thought of the glove she had dropped and resolved to get the other one off and send it after the first if possible.

Removing the right gauntlet, which was furthest from Mrs. Pollzoff's side had been comparatively easy, but slipping out of the other which was placed close to the rip-ring of her parachute and almost under the woman's nose, was a more dangerous undertaking, but Roberta wasn't built of the stuff that quits; she knew that a quitter never wins and a winner never quits, so she watched until her companion was leaning far enough forward so that the motion of the arm would not attract her attention. Fortunately for Roberta, the woman decided to dim the lights in the cock-pit, so she herself could not see so easily and must keep close to the control-board to watch the dials.

Slowly and cautiously, the girl wriggled her fingers until finally they were partly out of the gauntlet, then she managed to slip it along toward her right hand, hoping to draw it across her lap and throw it as she had the other. Just then, Mrs. Pollzoff tipped Nike's nose at a sharp angle and climbed swiftly for several minutes, then leveled and shut off her motor. By that time the smell of salt water permeated the air and Roberta was desperately anxious to get the glove over before they reached the shore line where it might be lost in the ocean. In this project Mrs. Pollzoff helped her by leaning far over her own side of the plane, searching beneath her, and Roberta clearly heard the pounding of the breakers. With a slight twist of her body she transferred the gauntlet to her right hand, and with a second flip of her fingers, sent it over the side.

Mrs. Pollzoff settled quickly back into her seat while the heavens were split with a million tongues of forked lightning, and after a breathless instant, a terrific crack of thunder boomed and crashed as if bent on the destruction of the whole universe.

CHAPTER VIII
THROUGH THE STORM

If Roberta had really been unconscious when the fury of the storm burst upon them, with the repeated cutting flashes of light and the thunder booming like a terrific bombardment all about the gallant little Nike, she would have come to if there was any life in her at all. She started up with a wild cry, then remembered instantly that she was supposed to be just coming out of a prolonged period of sleep, and so, strained forward on her straps, stared around as if she had no knowledge of anything which had transpired, and struggled to free herself from the belts that held her secure.

At first Mrs. Pollzoff was too fully occupied to pay any attention to the plane's real pilot, and the girl managed to take in the whole situation. The lightning revealed an endless surge of white rollers stretched row after row and piling themselves on top of one another as the gale lashed them like an escaped demon. Her first sensation was one of dismayed certainty that her second glove had gone into the raging water beneath them, so that its chances of being picked up were ruined; the tiny thing would never be recovered and the name printed indelibly on the stiff cuff would never be deciphered.

Twisting and wriggling to get free of her bonds, Roberta verified what she already suspected, that they were secured well out of her reach. The rain began to pour down on them in great sheets as if the heavens had suddenly opened and dumped the accumulation of years on the struggling machine. She managed to catch a glimpse of the indicators and saw that the tanks were well filled; the altimeter registered eight thousand feet but it was going lower with each jerk of the pointer. Whether the engine was functioning or not she couldn't tell, because the howling wind deadened every other sound as Nike tipped and spun like a helpless leaf.

"Let me loose," Roberta shrieked, but if Mrs. Pollzoff heard, she paid no attention, but battled with grim determination with the controls, endeavoring to climb above the tempest which was pressing down on them with such power that it seemed impossible for the plane to lift an inch.

"Let me fly her," the girl pleaded frantically, for she realized above everything else, that Mrs. Pollzoff was losing her head, and that their chances of getting out of the dilemma were growing more and more remote. She strained so far forward that her shoulder touched that of the woman, who whirled about angrily, her teeth bared like those of a snarling animal at bay.

"Get out of the way!" She shoved her back into the drenched seat and shook her fist in her face. "Stay where you are or I'll throw you out!" Roberta couldn't hear a word, but there was no mistaking the command. "If I can't get us out, the three of us will go down together. I won't have it said that you saved me." Again the clenched fist shot close to the girl's face, and probably if there had been a moment to waste, she would have been struck.

With a furious snarl, Mrs. Pollzoff turned her attention back to her job, and after a grilling ten minutes, Nike's nose began to lift slowly. The brave little plane climbed sturdily into the gale, which continued to fight every fraction of an inch gained. Ten minutes more and they struggled above the worst of the storm, then Mrs. Pollzoff took time to put the cover over the top of the machine. Before it was closed she scanned the heavens and waters as best she could, but there was no sign of another plane in the air or ship on the ocean. When the cover was finally in place, the cock-pit no longer acted as a space to fill and help drag them to destruction, but the rain beat on the top, and in spite of the lights Mrs. Pollzoff turned on both inside and outside, the lightning filled the whole atmosphere with its weird glow, changing the cheerful illumination to a ghastly, sulphurous hue.

Consulting the altimeter again, Mrs. Pollzoff forced the plane to climb higher, but there seemed to be no ceiling to the storm, and they could not get above its rage. The wind veered around until it was on Nike's tail, and its force drove her ahead at a terrific speed. Here the woman showed a bit more sense than before, by letting the tempest carry them forward instead of struggling against it. She also kept climbing, but at a gradual ascent. The tiny clock on the control-board ticked away two hours, but they seemed more like one hundred and twenty years than that many minutes to the imprisoned young girl. It was nearly morning and if they succeeded in coming through the storm, the first streaks of dawn would be flashing across the heavens in another hour. But that hour too went by bringing no hopeful rays of day to relieve the blackness. On and on they went, once the tank had to be replenished, and once the engine crackled alarmingly for a moment, but that was adjusted. Two hours later they had traveled nearly two hundred miles. It was still raining, but a bit of light was beginning to force its way through the darkness.

Mrs. Pollzoff stubbornly refused to release her prisoner or ask advice, although her hands trembled and her body quivered with terror and weariness under the continuous strain, but she did not say another word to the girl beside her, nor did Roberta waste her own strength to plead that she might be given the management of Nike. She could not help admire the indomitable grit of the woman even while she deplored the fact that such courage was misdirected.

Another hour dragged on before there was the faintest sign that they might win through if Nike could hang together through the awful beating she was getting. The rain pounded against her, the gale pressed her down spasmodically, tossed her up again like a plaything, but all the time shoved her forward. It seemed to the girl as if every section in her construction must surely be ripped apart any moment, and Roberta's heart was grateful for the skill and careful workmanship which had been put into her little craft.

The girl Sky-Pilot's head no longer ached from the effects of the drug, and her mind was clearer as she tried to figure how she might get free of her bonds, but whenever she wiggled too strenuously, Mrs. Pollzoff would look at her maliciously and glance at the buckles to be sure that they were where she had put them. Thinking of the construction of the plane brought back to Roberta's mind the fact that Mr. Wallace had installed an alarm button; one which was in some way tuned with the broadcasting band, and her heart leaped. Months before when the Blue Pirate Terror had been making a determined effort to force her out of the sky she had pressed her foot over one of the narrow boards in the flooring and by this means had released a spring carefully hidden. If she wasn't too far away from any broadcasting or radio station she might be heard again, but she knew that the other time she had used this emergency, dozens of men were listening for it and had instantly sprung into action.

Leaning over, as if weary, Roberta studied the floor for the tiny knot which marked the secret section, but the cloak Mrs. Pollzoff had used to dim the lights on the control board was over it. However, she knew well exactly where it was located, and although she had never released it from the passenger's seat, she repeated in her mind the directions. She must reach it with her heel and press hard with the side of it until she felt it give, then she was to hold it so a second, after which it was to be again released.

Roberta hadn't the faintest idea where they were, nor could she tell from the charts, for the compass was on the further side of the control-board and as Mrs. Pollzoff managed the machine her body obstructed the view. She feared they were so far away that it would do no good at all to use Mr. Wallace's clever little invention, but just because she was uncertain of the result she wasn't passing up even an uncertain effort which might help the searchers locate her. She moved her bound feet forward experimentally under the cloak, but although she tried pressing with her heel she found no spot which responded to the force. However, she might get a chance later, so she watched for an opportunity.

Another hour went by slowly, then Mrs. Pollzoff got out the container of food; poured herself a drink of strong coffee which she drank black, then took another. That steadied her nerves somewhat and she filled a cup for Roberta, but to this she added a quantity of milk and held it to the girl's lips. It had been in the thermos bottle and was a sickish warm, a nasty mixture, but she drank it gratefully, for her throat was dry as parchment, and her tongue swollen.

"Thank you," she said when the last drop was gone, but she didn't expect to be heard.

After that the woman got out more food, and between operations necessary to keep Nike balanced, she managed to feed the girl beside her some bread and butter sandwiches, topping them off with a little water poured from a tin container. The amount of food, water and the fact that arrangements had been made for the refueling in the air was convincing proof that the woman had carefully planned this scheme, but there was no fathoming the reason for it. When the meal was finished, what was left was stored away again, the cloak was folded, put out of the way, and Roberta's heart leaped hopefully.

It took the girl Sky-Pilot only a few moments to locate the tiny knot in the floor, which was still wet from the drenching it had received while the cover was open. The little square with its outline so dim it could barely be seen was inches away from her feet, and thanking her lucky star that Mrs. Pollzoff had not been able to secure her feet to the seat, she calculated its position. It was still raining, the wind was still blowing them forward and Roberta yawned wearily as she glanced at the shelter above them. Stretching her back, which was strained and aching in every muscle, she managed slowly to give her body a luxuriant treat by moving every part of it, including her feet. They went in the direction of the knot, but when she leaned forward a trifle she saw that it was not far enough.

At that moment Mrs. Pollzoff drew herself up in her own seat, leaned back to relax her pain-racked limbs, and then Roberta took advantage of the opportunity offered. She slid low, her feet extended as far as she could get them, and when she guessed that they were in the right spot, she pressed hard. But there was no yield, not the slightest movement, and she grew faint with discouragement. Then she reasoned that the water might have swollen the board, so she pressed again, throwing every ounce of her strength into that heel. Still it did not sink. Moving her foot a trifle she tried again, harder than ever and kept it up. At last the wee board gave slightly, so, with a heart beating furiously, she continued to push on it with all her strength. Anxiously she held the position for fully a minute, dreading every second that her companion might suspect some sort of trick, but apparently Mrs. Pollzoff was confident that her prisoner was helpless. Just then Nike began to buck, as if it was riding steep rollers, and the attention of his pilot was demanded.

"Get back, out of the way," she ordered harshly and gave the girl a shove.

Thankful that the command had been delayed so long, Roberta sat up quickly in her seat, her eyes swept the little square, and she saw it slip slowly into place. At least the signal was set and if only some government wireless man or anybody at all would pick it up and start inquiries as to its cause, they could tell at Lurtiss Field where Nike was and possibly trace her to her destination.

It was getting extremely cold, more so than the altitude would warrant unless they had been coming steadily north. To occupy her mind, Roberta tried to calculate how far they had come if they had followed the course the woman had set when they left Charleston, but there were so many "ifs" to the reasoning, that she couldn't get even an idea, so she gave it up. As soon as she could read the indicators she would be able to tell. Now she was tired, hopelessly so, and her heavy lids dropped over her eyes, but she forced herself to keep them open. Mrs. Pollzoff too, must be greatly fatigued; she couldn't stand such a strain indefinitely, and besides, unless they were refueled again, they would be compelled to make a landing very shortly.

In order to keep herself awake, Roberta went over carefully in her mind every detail of the days since that first morning when she and Nike had been engaged to take Mrs. Pollzoff on her mysterious mission. At first she had given her passenger little thought, but the seeming aimlessness of their flights, together with the woman's taciturnity had made her uneasy. She tried hard to recall anything she had done to offend the woman or arouse her animosity, but could recall nothing.

Again she tried to remember the words she had heard vaguely when she was sinking into unconsciousness, but they continued to elude her. She wondered if by any possible chance Mrs. Pollzoff had objected to young Powell's seeing them off, but promptly dismissed the idea as too absurd for consideration. Who could mind the appearance of the fun-loving chap and his sister? No, Roberta was sure that it was something that went back further, and again she racked her brain for the answer.

"At any rate, I guess she isn't interested in killing me or she would have done it long ago; she has had opportunity enough. She might have given me a second dose of drug, bigger than the other, and finished the job. If she had wanted to do anything of that kind, I certainly gave her a good chance when I ate and drank. Wonder why I wasn't afraid to take the food! I might have been afraid not to, I don't know. Heavens, I'd like to go to sleep, but I can't desert Nike—I won't," she resolved, but it was a resolution mighty difficult to keep.

No matter how long the engine stood up, the plane held together, and the fuel lasted; the woman was bound to reach a point when her body refused to act. Even now she was moving in jerks, staring three and four times at the different indicators before she was positive of the readings. Her breath came in painful gasps; Roberta could tell that by the way her shoulders heaved; she moved her feet as if they felt weighted, and twice her head nodded, but it was brought up always with a quick jerk. As soon as the woman's will power weakened, as it surely must, then Roberta was sure that she could manage to get free of her bonds. She could wriggle and twist until she could reach the buckle, and with one arm loose, the rest would be but the work of a moment; then she could take charge, and would see to it that Mrs. Pollzoff did not get the upper hand again.

As she glanced at the woman, whose fatigue was obvious, she determined to make a try for her freedom at once for it was probable that if Mrs. Pollzoff fainted from strain and exhaustion, she would get herself so tangled with the controls of the plane that before Roberta could get loose, Nike would have her nose buried in the bottom of the ocean, if it was still under them, or in the ground if they were traveling over land. After fifteen minutes, during which she moved her elbow not more than an inch at a time, the girl finally got her left hand back to the buckle, but maintaining the same position for so long a period had made her fingers so cold and numb that contact with the hard metal sent thousands of pins and needles stinging through her body. It took considerable time before the digits could feel with any accuracy, but at last they did. She could not risk a glance at what she was trying to do, but she felt the end of the strap, placed her fingers well over it, and slowly drew them back until there was a hump in the leather. Under this lee-way she pushed with her thumb, then working breathlessly she got the strap through the end of the buckle.

At that moment Mrs. Pollzoff leaned back as if she suspected something amiss and glanced at her companion, but her eyes were so heavy, and Roberta looked so much as if she were nearly asleep, that she devoted her energy to the job at hand, which was demanding enough. It was still raining, but not so violently, the wind blew with an angry roar as if furious with Nike for not being brought down in splinters, while intermittent flashes of lightning and a far off bombing of thunder kept them reminded that they were in the greatest danger, so the robber-pilot bent forward again. Three minutes later Roberta pushed the tongue of the buckle out of the hole.

Never had Roberta's heart hammered so furiously as it did while her fingers gradually got the strap through, but at last it was accomplished. She wriggled just enough to draw it under her back, which loosened her right arm. It had been tight so long that there was almost no sensation left, and as the blood began to circulate more normally the pain was excruciating. The belt had been wound about her arm in three twists, and being mighty careful that the strap across her body remained, to all appearances, as usual, she finally got it free. What should she do next was the question which immediately confronted her. She made up her mind that the best thing to do was to allow her body to relax as much as possible so that if she had to make a quick move, she would be able to manage. In the meantime, she might get an opportunity to free her feet.

With this project in mind, Roberta drew her feet back carefully, at the same time lowering her right hand. She was glad that the gauntlets had been removed, and wondered a little why Mrs. Pollzoff had not missed them. But she evidently didn't and that was something to be thankful for. It was half an hour before she finally brought her fingers into contact with the strap, the buckle of which was in the back, then drooping forward as if she were asleep, she gave a great sigh, and closed her lids, but her hand worked quickly and presently the strap was off. She couldn't prevent its dropping down, but she was banking on the fact that Mrs. Pollzoff had been paying no attention to her. Cautiously moving her toes and ankles, the girl slowly began to feel more normal. Although she was horribly weary, she determined that in a few minutes she would take charge of the situation. But a moment later, Mrs. Pollzoff shut off the engine and Nike began to glide down; whether it was to the earth or water, there was no telling, but she was coming down, and the pilot was evidently preparing to make a landing.

"If she does," Roberta thought, "she'll surely discover that I got loose."

CHAPTER IX
MAROONED

What was to happen when they finally landed, Roberta could not even guess, but she determined to be on the alert. She judged they had maintained a high altitude, and this fact was promptly verified as she watched Mrs. Pollzoff attend to the plane. Soon she took time to slide the cover from over the cockpit and all that could be seen was a thick fog which enveloped them. The woman scanned the earth beneath her and as she did that Roberta managed to catch a glimpse of the fuel indicator, the needle of which showed that they could go very little further.

The fact promptly banished a sudden idea of pushing the woman out and racing back into the heavens, for such a scheme would be foolhardy, inasmuch as Nike could carry her only a short distance. Her second plan depended greatly upon what happened when the plane's wheels touched the ground, if they did, but Roberta made ready to snatch any opportunity which offered itself. She hated to abandon the machine; that would have to be her last resort, for she realized that the woman wasn't coming down any place where she did not expect to find friends and accommodations. Carefully drawing up her right hand, she found the latch to the door at her side, and at the same time got loose her safety strap so that it could not hold her back.

The chute would also hamper any quick movement, but before she could manage to rid herself of the awkward bulky thing, Nike touched ground.

A few feet away was a huge fire, which looked as if it had been built as a beacon for the woman, but even its blaze was veiled by the swirling fog which surrounded it. As the plane curved, its wheels bumped first one side, then the other; once they struck something so large that they jumped, so Mrs. Pollzoff was fully occupied in bringing the machine to a stop. Blurred figures of men moved between them and the fire, and at last when Nike stopped, they came forward. There was a confused murmur of voices.

"Hurry and help me," Mrs. Pollzoff snapped, but her voice cracked shrilly.

"We're here—"

"Been waitin' fer hours," snapped one who seemed in charge of the party. "Keeping this fire going. What kept you?"

"Think I could do any better through that storm—"

"Aw, that's it, eh? Flew yourself. The boss said you'd probably try that fool trick."

"What was the matter with the girl doing it—she'd have—"

"Shut your fool mouth. Get her out and be quick about it, you think she's so wonderful—" Mrs. Pollzoff swore roundly.

"She'd have done it quicker. It's only fool's luck that you didn't have a smash-up."

"Get her out—" Mrs. Pollzoff stamped her feet furiously.

"Did you kill her?" One of the men came close to the woman, and his tone was threatening. "You'll get yours from the boss if she's hurt; he needs her in this business and you had your orders."

"I tell you she's all right, only asleep. Get her out. We're both nearly dead."

But Roberta didn't wait to hear anything more. She threw her weight against the door, jumped out under the shelter of Nike's wing, and leaped into the dense fog. Instantly three men who had been coming around the plane, sprang toward her. There followed a wild scramble of feet as the girl ran desperately from the scene, but the chute interfered, although she tried hard to get out of it as she fled.

"Bring up some of those torches," one of the men bellowed. "She can't get far."

Immediately a dozen firebrands were being brandished through the fog, in a moment her footprints were discovered and panting men rushed in pursuit. The rough ground, the unwieldy chute, and her own weariness were almost too much for the fleeing girl, but she pushed on as fast as she could, hoping to find some place into which she could dodge, and trying to plant her feet on rocks which would leave no tell-tale trail. It was amazing that she managed to keep going so long, but suddenly the leader of the men caught sight of her.

"You ain't going to be hurt, Miss, and you're headin' out to sea," he called, and although his voice was rough, there was nothing in it to fear. Just at that moment a wave splashed over Roberta's ankles, verifying the last part of his statement; but a wave of discouragement even larger and more formidable than the water piled over her, completely dispelling every hope of escape.

"Oh, please," she cried—but that was all she could say, for her head seemed ready to burst open with pain, sharp daggers stung her eyes, and just as the man reached her, her body grew limp.

"That wild cat gave you a hard time," he remarked as he picked her up in his arms, but what he said or did was lost to the girl, for she had fainted dead away. It was lucky he was there, because she would have slumped into the water, been tossed helplessly on the in-coming tide, and no one could have saved her from being crushed among the rocks.

Being a healthy girl the state of unconsciousness did not last long and a bit later she opened her eyes again. A dark woman, who looked like an Indian had her in charge; while one of the men stood ready with a flask, some of the contents of which was still stinging her throat. Her flying suit had been opened and she was stretched out on a rough bed of boughs, and another Indian, a younger one, unfastened her shoes. It wasn't a comforting sight, but it was evident that every one of them was bent on bringing her to and making her as comfortable as possible.

"Here, that's the girl! Take a bit more of this and it will knock the kinks out of you," the man urged. He was the man who had picked her up, and there was a smoldering light in his eyes as if, regardless of what the situation might really be, his sympathies were with Roberta.

"I'm lots better," she managed to gasp. "Thank you so much."

"Sure, but you'll be better still. Come along, this won't hurt you, and you surely do need it. The natives will do the little things to help you." He went over with the flask and Roberta obeyed without further protest. Her good sense told her that she must do everything possible to regain her strength if she expected to get away from the place. She wanted to ask where she was, but decided it might be better to wait until she was more sure of herself and those around her.

"I ain't never been in favor of this kidnaping business, Wat," said one of the men who was standing by. "It always sets the crowd against you."

"Well, keep your shirt on, Slim," Wat answered under his breath. "Better yell fer some of that soup," he added.

"Come along with the soup," Slim shouted.

"Think I'm at the Pole." A third man appeared with a tin of steaming soup, which the woman took from him.

"That's good. Let Nomie feed you a little at a time, and if they don't treat you right, yell for Wat and I'll come running." He grinned down at her, then spoke to Nomie, who nodded that she understood, but Roberta didn't catch the words.

"Good," said Nomie, as she sniffed the contents of the bowl. Then she took a crust of hard bread, dipped it into the liquid. "Too hot," she told Roberta. "Eat little from crust."

It was an odd way of taking nourishment, but Roberta was glad that she wasn't required to sit up and eat, for although the brandy she had swallowed was tingling warmly, she was woefully tired and making any sort of physical effort seemed impossible. The "soup" tasted of clams and milk, and she thought she had never eaten anything better. Conscientiously Nomie fed her, a little at a time, until finally it was cooler and she used a spoon instead of the bread, but she did not hasten the performance. The men had withdrawn tactfully to the other side of the huge bon-fire which was being raked into a smaller space as it was no longer needed as a beacon. Roberta wondered dully how it had helped Mrs. Pollzoff to know where to come down, but just then she saw Slim passing with a bundle of rockets and understood that the gang must have been shooting them intermittently while they waited, and more frequently when they heard the plane roaring toward them out of the fog.

"More bye and bye," Nomie said at last, and she handed the dish to the young girl. "Fix bed, Natell," she added. The Indian girl hurried away, and presently Wat returned.

"Feel able to walk?" he asked gruffly.

"Guess so," Roberta answered. She managed to get to her feet, and although she felt better, she was still wobbly.

"Give her a hand there," Wat ordered.

"Good," agreed Nomie and she slipped her strong arm about Roberta's waist. "This way." They proceeded slowly away from the fire, and presently, a few yards ahead, she saw a small blaze through the fog.

"Here you are!" Natell was standing in a low doorway.

"Now, get some sleep. Nobody's going to hurt you," Wat said quietly, and the two native women helped her stumble inside.

Roberta was too weary to pay much attention to anything, except that the room she entered appeared to be a long, low one with many bright colored draperies hanging on the wall. In a moment she was led to a rude bed, the top of which was piled high with pillows, and as she seated herself on the edge, she saw another one a few feet away. Across the top of it lay Mrs. Pollzoff, already sound asleep. Nomie and her young daughter made short work of helping their charge out of a part of her clothes, but they hadn't finished, when her weary lids closed over her eyes as she fell asleep.

Although she had no idea what time it was when she opened her eyes again, the girl Sky-Pilot had slept around the clock. The Indians had certainly made her very comfortable among the huge pillows, and now she yawned and stretched luxuriously. Turning over she saw that close to the bed the girl, Natell, was seated, her small brown hands busily darting back and forth over a piece of weaving. Her keen ears must have been alert for a sound from her charge, for she immediately called shrilly. "No-mee, No-mee!" Nomie came at once and glanced at the blinking young pilot.

"Good," she greeted soberly.

"She is awake," announced Natell.

"Of course I am awake, but—" A bit of the recollection of the horrors through which she had gone, returned to her mind, and instinctively she glanced toward the second bed where she had seen Mrs. Pollzoff recovering from her own exhaustion, but the woman wasn't there and the bed had been smoothed. As far as she could tell there was no one in the room but the natives and herself. "Where am I? I mean, what is this place?" she asked curiously.

"Island," Nomie answered. She was getting the white girl's clothes out of a queer sort of chest that looked as if it had been made of pieces of driftwood. As the woman showed no inclination of imparting more information, Roberta decided that it might be the better part of wisdom to be content with what she had learned.

"Fine!" Natell spread the garments before their owner with true feminine interest, and in another moment, Nomie produced the traveling bag from behind one of the curtains, as well as the wrist watch they had taken off to add to her comfort while she slept. The time-piece was going but Roberta stared at it in amazement, for it showed less than two hours later than the hour they had landed.

"How long did I sleep?" she asked quickly.

"One sun," Nomie smiled at her.

"Good sleep," Natell added, with a wide grin.

"I should say so," Roberta replied laughing. She had a hunch that it might be greatly to her advantage to be as friendly as possible with the people of the island, because recalling the dialogue which had passed between Wat and Slim after the arrival of Nike, their attitude toward her abduction, or kidnaping was one of strong disapproval. The native women, too, were kindly disposed and Roberta wondered to what tribe they belonged. She had seen any number of American Indians in the United States and in Canada also, when she was touring with the Wallaces, but while the two who were caring for her had high cheek bones, dark eyes, and skin, they looked as if they belonged to another race entirely. While she put on her clothes, Nomie was fussing about a small oil stove, and presently the odor of coffee permeated the dwelling. Ready at last she noticed that Natell's eyes were attracted by a string of red beads among the articles in the tray of her bag.

"Eat," invited Nomie.

"You may have these," Roberta picked up the beads and fastened the strand about the younger girl's neck.

"No, no, no," she said quickly, and glanced with evident anxiety around the room as if she expected someone to step out.

"What?" demanded Nomie coming to the girl.

"See." Natell looked wistfully at her mother, who also took a hasty glance over her shoulder.

"Please let her keep them!" Roberta pleaded. "If you do not want anyone to know I gave them to her, slip them out of sight. I have more. See!" She pointed to other ornaments in her bag, and after a few words exchanged in their own tongue, Nomie nodded her head.

"Good," she agreed, and immediately Natell fixed the neck of her homespun dress so that the treasure could not be seen. Her mother drew a chair, cut from the stump of a tree, before an equally primitive table and spread out a meal of cornbread, fish and coffee. To this she added, surreptitiously, as if as a special treat, a tablespoonful of honey.

"Thank you very much," Roberta said, for she had an idea that the settlement did not boast of very much of the sweet.

"Good," the woman replied, but she kept her eyes on the door while Natell stood just outside of it until the girl Sky-Pilot had consumed the delicacy.

Roberta wondered why the great secrecy and reached the conclusion that Nomie's general orders had been that she was to do nothing more than absolutely necessary for the prisoner. When the meal was finished, she rose to go outside partly because the place was stuffy, and partly because she wanted to know if she were to be kept within certain limits. Neither of the natives made any move to detain her and once beyond the low entrance her first thought was for Nike, but the plane was nowhere in sight.

The day was clear and in front of the dwelling the rocky land sloped toward the water. Here and there were stretches of white sand, washed up by the high tides, and a bit further back the girl could see a few clusters of shrubs and trees whose sturdy trunks were bent and twisted as if they had maintained their place despite the gales which had beaten them without mercy. Walking slowly toward the edge of the Island, she paused to look back and then discovered that there was really no house; that the entrance was cut or dug from the face of a low cliff, nor was there a sign of another habitation.

Roberta's next thought was to find tracks of her machine, but she didn't, nor did she come across any blackened spot which the bon-fire had left. Trying to reconstruct the place from when she landed on it she discovered that the highwater mark came to within a few yards of the cliff, and calculating quickly she figured that there had been at least two changes in the tide while she slept, so all marks would be completely obliterated.

As there appeared to be no one to object to her walking about wherever she chose, the girl proceeded slowly along the edge of the beach, which was rugged and irregular. Locating the position of the sun did not help her reach any solution to the question of where she was marooned, but a bit later when she climbed to the top of a hill she knew without doubt that she was on an island; and because of the coldness in the air and the course Mrs. Pollzoff had set when they left Charleston, she was positive that she was pretty far north. How far, she had no way of telling. Every few minutes she scanned the sky for a glimpse of Nike or a rescuing plane, but the heavens were as empty as the vast expanse of sea that surrounded her.

Figuring the time since anyone she knew had heard of or from her the girl Sky-Pilot felt positive that a search of some kind must be already started. She had no hope of the second glove's having been found, but if the first one was picked up and passed on to any authority, at least they would have something upon which to work. Then, if Mr. Wallace's invention had not failed, and had been heeded, the men of Lurtiss field would certainly have further assistance in finding her. Again she looked about for a trace of the gallant little plane, but found nothing.

"Wonder if anyone has gone up in her," she remarked to herself. Then she wondered where Mrs. Pollzoff had gone. She guessed that the woman was not on this particular island, anyway, then suddenly she sat down and chuckled. "I'll bet she's gone off in Nike, and if she has, that little buzzer will be her Waterloo, for with the spring down, it will start again whenever the plane is taken into the air. Wouldn't it be topping if Mrs. Pollzoff gets herself caught!" But, although the idea was certainly amusing, Roberta sighed. "She's got too much sense, anyway, to go flying over the country in Nike—she'll know everyone will be on the lookout for the machine."

134

CHAPTER X
TREACHERY

The realization that Mrs. Pollzoff was too clever a woman to permit herself to be so easily caught ruined the tiny bit of fun Roberta had found in days. For minutes she stood, staring out at the sea and trying desperately to convince herself that she would soon find a way to escape. At first the fact that she were allowed to go about without guards and not kept under cover appeared to be a good thing, but as she thought that over, she made up her mind that this particular island was so far away from any line of travel or settlement that her captors had no fear of her being found by plane or boat; and she couldn't get away, so they were safe in letting her roam at will.

"No one would take Nike up," she said aloud because it was pleasant to hear something beside the ceaseless splash of the water on the shore. "Then," she added a bit later, "perhaps it's still here." The abode of Nomie was built in a rock so that anyone passing would not notice that it was a habitation; so perhaps a similar hiding place had been found for her plane.

Hopefully she set out again, and this time she investigated every high rock, shrub, clump of trees, and low cliff. For an hour she continued the search, and although she half skirted the island, there was little difference in the scene from one point to another. The sameness of it all was appallingly dreary. She tried hard to keep thoughts of her mother and father out of her mind, for she knew just how anxious and worried they must be. She could picture them listening for the familiar roar of the machine which would announce her return; running to the telephone every time it rang, eager for news that didn't come; hurrying to the door when the mail-man whistled, only to be disappointed when he brought no card or letter. Dad was doubtlessly making brave efforts to assure his wife that their daughter was quite safe—perhaps even fibbing a bit in an effort to make it easier. He had probably already got in touch with Mr. Trowbridge and her former flying-mates had been urged to keep an eye out for their girl Sky-Pilot, as they had dubbed her.

All those things made her heart sick and she wandered on and on hardly noticing where she went and twice she had to scramble up over rocks to get out of water into which her stumbling feet had taken her. At last, utterly weary and discouraged, she sank down on a hard wide stretch of sand and buried her head on her arm. Although she was nearly overcome with discouragement she did not give way to tears, for she knew they wouldn't help any. There was nothing she could do but wait, no matter how long it was. She sat quietly for a quarter of an hour and felt more rested, then a sort of plan formed itself in her mind. She must find out just where she was! With that information she might discover a way to escape. But with that encouraging idea, into her brain popped a hopeful thought that she would probably be watched to some extent and any move she made would be immediately reported. As she sat there feeling desperately lonely, she heard a gruff voice a short distance further on and recognized the man Wat, but could not see him.

"Well, I've fixed her up, just as you want, but whether you like it or not, I'm telling you it's no good. My advice—"

"I'm not asking you for your advice." That harsh voice was none other than Mrs. Pollzoff's.

"You're gettin' it gratis, see! When the Boss finds out how you balled up the works you're going to get plenty, I don't care how much of a drag you have with him. He told you what to do and you didn't do as he ordered—"

"Will you shut up!" The woman screamed.

"No, I won't. You haven't got a leg to stand on—"

"I tell you the girl was having us spied on—"

"You can tell me all you like, but I don't believe it, see? Now, this stunt you want to pull is a fizzle—and you'll get thrown as sure as you're born. You were told to stay here and look after the girl—"

"How do you know so much about what I was told?"

"That's an easy one. I was told that when the pair of you got here you'd stay, see, so I know those were your orders. If you found you were spied on, you had your orders to go on to Miami and keep away from here, and you were to keep out of the pilot seat. Instead of that you signaled that you were coming along O.K. and it wasn't until the re-fill that anyone knew you were at the controls—"

"I brought the plane through, didn't I? And I gave the fellows that were spying on us the slip, didn't I?" There was proud defiance in her tone.

"I'm not so sure that you did. You got here, yes, with the girl almost dead, and you flew the plane to satisfy your own conceit—"

"This plane belongs to me, understand, I'm doing what I please with it and you are obeying my orders regarding it! Bear that in mind. I made up my mind I was going to have it the first time I rode in it, if I had to steal it."

"Yes!" Wat remarked without much interest.

"Yes. Now I've got it, it's mine, I'm keeping it in payment for the buckshot that girl's father peppered on my chin. As long as there is the faintest sign of a scar, I'll feel they are still in my debt." She spoke with such passion that Roberta gasped in amazement and horror.

"Yes. Well, all I've got to say is that it's a pity her father had such darned poor aim—." Just then an engine roared and cut off further remarks, and Roberta leaped to her feet, for she recognized Nike's thunder. A moment later it rounded a curve and came rushing swiftly along the hard stretch of beach.

"Oh, they have painted her white," the girl gasped. Sure enough, Nike, all her own beautiful trimming concealed under the color which would make her hardest to pick out in the sky, was rushing forward swiftly, gaining speed at every turn of her whirling propeller. With an exclamation of dismay, Roberta started to run across the beach to her beloved machine and at that moment, Mrs. Pollzoff saw her. The woman's expression grew uglier than anything the girl had ever seen in her life and with a lurch Nike was spun around sharply; it was tearing after her and in another minute she would be cut to pieces in that cruel wheel. The plane's nose was pointed directly at the girl, rushing like some maddened demon to destroy her. There was no time to think or act. The only thing she could do was drop flat on her face and pray.

"God help me," formed on her lips, but before the words were out of her mouth, she felt something brush the full length of her body and knew that the machine had lifted before it touched her and was already two feet in the air. "Thank you," she sighed gratefully then raised her head lest Mrs. Pollzoff discover that by a miracle her fiendish plan had failed, and turn back to finish it, but Nike was climbing at top speed and was half way across the island.

"Hurt, Miss?" Wat came running.

"Thank you, no," she told him.

"You're mighty lucky." His rough face was white through its tan and to relieve his feelings, he shook his fist after the racing plane and its pilot.

"I hope you fly to perdition," he shouted.

"Second the motion," Roberta added, then she began to laugh hysterically and Wat stared down at her.

"Sure you're all right?" he asked again.

"Positive," she told him.

"You sure got a good guardian angel!"

"You don't seem overly fond of Mrs. Pollzoff."

"I don't know anyone who is," he replied.

"Did you paint Nike—the plane?" she ventured to ask.

"Yes," he admitted. "She's got money in these works so I had to, because she told me to, but it was a hurry-up job just on the outside. It's hardly dry yet, but that flying fool couldn't wait."

"She did appear to be in a hurry," the girl remarked.

Roberta didn't say so, but he had given her the information she wanted. They had not taken time to go over the inside of the machine and it was possible that the signal buzzer would be heard by someone. The girl wanted awfully to ask Wat where they were, but decided against being too inquisitive.

"I see the kid, Natell, over on the hill. Guess it's time you got something more to eat," he told her.

"That would be welcome," Roberta replied with a smile. She started toward the young Indian girl, but Wat called.

"I say, Miss Langwell!"

"Yes." She turned about.

"Thought I'd tell you it's about three hundred miles, air line, to the nearest coast."

"Three hundred miles!" she exclaimed in dismay.

"Yah, kind of a long stretch when you figure doing it on a raft fer instance, or a canoe," he added.

"I hadn't been thinking of a raft," she grinned.

"Reckon not, but you might. Building one would be a real good way to fill in your time, if you're a good hand with a hammer, but don't set no store by it."

"As a hammerer I'm bad, but I might have tried it. Thanks so much for the tip."

"Keep it for what it's worth," he replied and strode off in the opposite direction.

Hurrying toward the waiting Natell, the girl Sky-Pilot's step was light for she felt that after all its seeming hopelessness, the hours had not been devoid of results. She had learned that Wat and his companions were located on the opposite side of the island, that Mrs. Pollzoff had gone off in the repainted Nike, whose nose pointed east when she disappeared on the horizon, which meant that the nearest point of land was probably that way, three hundred miles. Recalling her maps and large bodies of water in the north, she wondered if the island was in the Bering Sea. If it was, the mainland must be Alaska, United States territory.

If she wasn't west of Alaska the island might be in one of the large bodies to the north of Canada, but that wouldn't make a bit of difference, for every pilot, worthy of the name, was a citizen of the world, and the sudden disappearance of one in any part of the globe immediately aroused the interest of every land. It was a mighty comforting thought and Roberta was humming a little tune when she joined Natell, who looked at her with wide eyes.

"That wooden bird could not destroy you," she said as if she could hardly believe the evidence of her own optics.

"No." Roberta was about to explain that while she might have been cut to shreds, the plane hadn't really touched her, but then she recalled reading that Indians have many superstitions and if they believed that she was favored by the Gods or had a charmed life, they might be inveigled into helping her escape. She had also read that the natives succeeded in traveling with their frail crafts over waters a white man, unless driven by desperation, would refuse to attempt; and safely reach ports unbelievably distant. The pair reached the dug-out and the young girl immediately started to speak swiftly to her mother in their own tongue and the girl Sky-Pilot guessed that the older woman was getting the details of the miraculous escape of their white charge. Nomie's own eyes widened during the recital and at its close, she crossed herself piously.

"Eat," she invited.

"Thank you."

The evening meal consisted of reindeer meat, dried potatoes baked in a sort of pancake form, cornbread which was whiter than that she had eaten earlier in the day, coffee sweetened with canned milk, and a paste of dried fruits. The girl was mighty hungry and she ate her full share, but she watched that she did not overstep the bounds of good breeding. She realized that probably every mouthful had to be brought at regular intervals, not too close together, from the distant mainland and that the rations of Nomie and Natell were necessarily doled out with care so the supplies would not be depleted before they could be replenished. The food tasted good and Nomie seemed to appreciate the fact that her guest or prisoner was not too finical.

Glancing about the primitive living quarters, Roberta thought of her mother and recalled long ago days when she was a little girl, with a little girl's likes and dislikes for different foods. Then, Mrs. Langwell had told her if she would learn to eat anything put before her, when she grew up she would save herself all sorts of unpleasant experiences and keep from being classified by her friends as too much of a nuisance to have around when they were inviting guests.

"It's a mighty good thing Mom taught me that," she said to herself, "for I certainly have landed in all sorts of places, been given all sorts of things to eat, and it has always been jolly." She thought of "Pa and Ma Perkins," into whose treacherous "backyard" she had brought the Wallace's when she was flying blind through a bad fog.

But it wasn't possible, in the face of her present dilemma to keep her mind on experiences of the past and as she thought of what she had seen of the island Roberta wondered if there was any sort of wireless station on it. She hadn't seen anything like an antenna, but it seemed hardly possible that the men stationed here had no means of communicating with the outside world. Immediately she began to think seriously of the radio. One of the men had said that Mrs. Pollzoff had signaled that all was O.K. when she was flying toward them. She must have carried some sort of instrument which she had used, but, rack her brain as hard as she could, Roberta couldn't recall a moment when a communication had been sent out. To be sure it might have been done when she was unconscious; also it might have been done on Nike's radio, but that was not equipped to send. If a station picked her up there were certain signals she could send, a sort of code; also, if Mr. Wallace's special apparatus was sprung, she could reply to questions, but in order to do that she had to press a switch, which looked like one of the screws on the dial-board. This fact was known to only a few officials inside and outside of the Lurtiss organization; Mrs. Pollzoff was ignorant of their existence, so she could not very well avail herself of them.

The girl Sky-Pilot resolved that on the following day she would search for a radio. Ever since she could remember, Harvey had built them, so she grew up with more than an average understanding of their construction and operation; also, she had learned more during her period of training at Lurtiss Field for Mr. Wallace considered that a pilot who did not understand sending and receiving, as well as rig-up, was only half trained. Now, if she could locate a set here she would watch for an opportunity to send out an S.O.S. But she would have to find out first where she was located; just saying that she was on an island which she thought was in the Bering Sea would not be much help. Not only the Bering Sea but every large body of water had numberless uncharted islands and this particular one was probably chosen by the Boss, whoever he was, because of its location and apparent barrenness.

When the meal was finished Roberta offered to help Nomie, but she was brushed aside, although not unkindly, so she went out again. The sun was still high and the girl realized that because she was a good way north there would be a great difference in the length of the days and nights, and she wondered if she would see any of the marvelous coloring and brilliant spectacles of which she had read, but the heavens were clouding over, and far in the horizon she discovered a mist which looked very much like a gathering fog.

"Hope it isn't going to be as thick as it was the other day when we landed," she remarked, and as she knew a great deal about the density and speed of the all-enveloping mists, she kept her eye on it to be sure that she did not wander too far away. Recalling the treachery of the shore line she had no doubt that she could very quickly lose herself. Observation was also a branch of an aviator's training, besides it was a part of Roberta's nature, so as she walked slowly in the opposite direction from that she had taken earlier in the day, she carefully noted every rock, counted her steps when she crossed smooth stretches, and turned about frequently so that she would be familiar with the appearance of the landscape when she returned.

She had been walking nearly an hour by her watch, which she had kept running although she knew the time must be different on the Island than it was at home, when she noticed a hill which rose gradually a short distance in front of her. The fog was coming in, but she was sure she could manage to get back safely, so she proceeded until she was standing on the top. There she discovered that it extended in a long, narrow plateau which seemed almost straight, but as she went along she saw that it curved slightly toward the water. The wind was blowing so cold that she wrapped her coat around her tightly and decided to go on and see what it was like on the other side. The surface was not entirely flat; in places it dipped slightly, as if worn down by storms, and in a couple of sections were wide cracks, such as those made by ice in the crevices of rocks.

The whole flat was deadly monotonous and Roberta was about to return before she was caught in the fog, when suddenly, as if from beneath her feet, she heard a confusion of strange sounds. Breaking the island's solitude as it did, it made her jump, and then, controlling her nerves, she paused to listen. It seemed to her as if it was some kind of an animal, then after a moment she wondered if it could be a baby, but she instantly dismissed that idea. Walking back carefully to the widest crack she had crossed, she bent over to hear better, then got down on her stomach to see what might be there. It occurred to her that some young animal might have fallen through and was unable to climb out; it might be hurt and she could help it. But the crevice was dark and then she heard the noises again and distinguished voices. Quickly she pressed her ear close, then jumped, for a hand was laid on her shoulder.

CHAPTER XI
A FIGHT IN THE NIGHT

That hand gripping her shoulder made Roberta's heart skip a beat, but after a moment when it didn't yank her to her feet she gathered courage to look around. To her great relief she saw that it was Nomie.

"Fog coming," the Indian said, scarcely above a whisper.

"I'll come," Roberta answered quickly and rose to her feet. Her companion put her fingers over her lips, which the girl understood to mean that they must keep very quiet, then the pair hurried stealthily across the plateau. When they were well below the hill, Nomie paused, her face very sober.

"Keep way from cracks," she said briefly.

"I thought it was a baby animal of some kind. I was going to help it up if I could," she explained and Nomie looked at her searchingly. "That is true," Roberta added emphatically.

"Good," Nomie appeared relieved and willing to believe the story, but she went on. "Noises you hear, things you know not, pay no heed to. I give you leave to walk; you will make me trouble—"

"I'll be mighty careful," Roberta put in hastily. "You have been very good to me and I appreciate it."

"Speak not of the noise or the crack," the woman urged.

"Not a word to anyone."

"Busy yourself with watching the sky," was the woman's advice.

"All right," she promised, but her mind was endeavoring to solve the mystery of the plateau.

Roberta thought it might be the living quarters of Wat and the men, but if that was all, why had Nomie been so fearful? There was certainly something going on under those rocks which was a secret that was guarded with extreme care and if it had been one of the men who had discovered her trying to fathom it, things might go very hard with her. From what the Indian woman said, the white girl gathered that she was expected to keep a close watch on her prisoner, and an exhibition of too much inquisitiveness would surely cost her what liberty she enjoyed. Presently they reached the dug-out, and after watching the woman gather some bits of driftwood from the beach, they went inside.

"Go to bed," Nomie said quietly. "Sleep very sound," she added "You be sick if get no rest."

"I'm not tired," Roberta answered, but there was something in the woman's eyes which seemed to plead with her to obey, so greatly puzzled, she added, "Not very tired, but I believe I'll feel better if I lie down for a while."

"Good," the woman answered. "Just like you are, lie down," She tugged at the pillows piled on the corner bed, and guessing that she was to be hidden, Roberta stretched herself among them. A moment later anyone coming into the room, unless they knew that she was there, would not have noticed her.

For minutes Roberta lay still as a mouse, every nerve tense to know what was going to happen, but as the time went on and she did not hear anything more than the splashing of the waves against the rocks outside, the drip of heavy fog, which had rolled in thickly, and the Indian woman moving about the dug-out, her mind leaped back to the discovery of the crack on the plateau, and to wondering what the mystery could be. Then, suddenly she heard a whining noise, something like the sounds beneath the rocks, followed by a gruff barking and snorting, which could not belong to a dog. It kept up for an hour, then seemed to die down, and, because effects of the strain she had been through had not entirely worn off, her eyelids closed and she drifted off to sleep, but not quite soundly enough to make her absolutely oblivious of her surroundings. Into her lulled brain leaped a train of thoughts, half dream and half reality. The past and the present, the possible and the impossible in a conglomeration of fancies, but suddenly her eyes popped wide open and every faculty was alert.

The first thing she saw was Nomie standing near the bed, but her head was turned toward the door and her body was stiff, as if she anticipated some great danger. Not daring to move, Roberta listened, then she heard the unmistakable scraping of a boat on the rocks as if it were being shoved high to prevent its being taken out by the tide. This was followed by men's gruff voices, and finally the sound of stamping feet making their way to the Indian's house. Just then a distant voice hailed the newcomers, and Nomie said something scarcely above a whisper to Natell, who jumped up from the other side of the room, hurried across to her mother and then quickly parting the nearest heavy draperies, the young girl disappeared.

From out on the darkening beach there came the sound of an exchange of calls, then it seemed to Roberta as if the man who had greeted the boatmen must have joined them, for his voice was mingled with the others. All that she could make out of the conversation was its punctuation of oaths, and while this was going on, Nomie stepped stealthily to the door, got back of it and started to close it, but it was made of heavy timbers and did not move easily. Just as she was about to give it the last shove, a great boot was stuck over the sill, and a drunken voice brawled.

"Gwan, No-mee, none of that. Give me something to drink!"

"Got none," she answered.

"Sure you have. Come across with it quick."

"Got none," she repeated. "Go Wat for some. He keeps," she answered. "Go way, you get killed the Boss find you here."

"Sure I will, but he's too far away to find me," the man laughed wickedly, then shouted to the others, "Come on! Nomie's trying to hold out on us! Give me a hand!"

"Say, don't do that! The Boss will be mad as anything and you know the last time you smashed things he told you that after the next spree he'd kill you! You were on your knees with the barrel of gun in your mouth." The man who was speaking was the one who had called, so Roberta judged that he must be a member of the group on the island.

"Well, tell her to open the door. I'm not going to smash anything. I want some coffee; the woman can make me some." The voice was considerably less belligerent, but the fellow was just intoxicated enough to be stubborn.

"Go back to the boat and get your own cook to make you a barrel of coffee. Let the woman alone, I tell you, or I'll send for Wat."

"Yes, you'll send fer Wat—well, who'll you send, Brick Top, one of my crew? I'll shoot the first man that stirs a leg."

"Now, look here, Cap, you get back in the boat and go about your business, and I won't say a word about seeing you here. If you don't beat it, you're going to make trouble for your whole crew. Go on back and sleep it off, then come over and get the cargo," Brick Top urged.

"Come along, Cap, he's givin' you good talk. If you don't, we'll take the boat and pull back without you, see?" That was one of the crew, and others of its members, evidently not caring to share in the captain's punishment if he persisted in disobeying, backed him up quickly. In a moment by the sounds, Cap was being led meekly away, but suddenly his voice rose again.

"I'm not going to my ship till I say how-de-do to Nomie. I ain't landing on her shore an' goin' off 'sif I ain't a gentleman." Then followed a scuffle and soon the Cap, leering broadly, had forced his way into the house. "Ain't goin' 'way—"

"Get him away," Nomie shrieked.

"Aw, shut up, woman. Bible says women should keep still. You're makin' too much noise—"

"Come out of there," Brick Top snapped angrily.

"Blowed if I do," retorted the Cap, and with a powerful swing of his arm, the back of his hand struck Brick Top such a resounding blow that he reeled across the room. "You're like Nomie, you say too much with your mouth." But the younger man recovered himself quickly and sprang at the drunken captain.

"You fool," he roared furiously, "will you get out?"

"No," Cap bellowed, mightily encouraged by the success of his first attack. "And no blasted redhead's going to make me."

"No? Well, you'll change your tune," Red snapped.

"Come on, Cap," one of the crew urged. They were crowding in the door, and one of them tried to catch the captain's collar, but he lolled aside, then, with head down like a charging bull, he rushed at the smaller man, caught him about the waist, lifted him in the air and would have broken his back in another moment if Nomie hadn't thrown a kettle which struck him in the head. This dazed him for an instant so that his hold was broken and Red wriggled out of his grasp, but his tight-fitting fur cap saved the captain from more serious damage.

"Oh, you'll hit me from behind," he howled, believing Red responsible for the blow. He leaped at the young fellow and immediately the pair were in the throes of such a violent conflict that it did not seem possible that either of them could come out alive. They crashed in first one corner then the other with lightning speed, and as Roberta heard and caught glimpses of the horrible spectacle she was nearly overcome with nausea. She thought that any moment the built-in bed would be ripped from the wall to which it was fastened and she wondered dully why none of the crew interfered. Then she found herself trying to calculate just how long it would be before the courageous little Red would be reduced to an unrecognizable mass of flesh.

It occurred to the girl Sky-pilot that it was because of her presence that Red had so strenuously objected to the captain's entering the dugout, and thinking back, she believed that

Nomie must have sighted the boat on the water. That would explain her reason for wanting the white girl out of sight when the small boat came ashore with the men whose rough temper was well known to her. By that time the two bodies crashed against the foot of the bed and a huge hand clutched the pillows to keep him from falling, but Cap's foot slipped on the wet floor. He flung himself up with all his strength, clutched at the upright support, but under his weight the sapling gave way, the corner of the bed came down with its pile of protecting pillows cascading into the room. Quick as a flash, Roberta rolled to the further side, but the tumbling piece of furniture prevented her from keeping out of sight, so she was forced to get to her feet close to the wall, what was left of the bed—rolling in front of her. Just as Cap raised his ugly head and caught sight of her terrified white face, the huge form of Wat rushed in and hurled forward, the man's legs whipped about the captain's body like a powerful vise, one hand snatched back the fur hat while the other brought the butt end of a gun down on the man's head so hard that he was immediately knocked unconscious. During the last part of the fight, the curious crew had crowded into the room, and now Wat turned on them. Beyond the door, Roberta caught a glimpse of Slim and other familiar faces, set grimly, while the barrel of more than one gun was in evidence.

"What are you fellows doing here?" he demanded sharply.

"Cap ordered us to bring him over," the nearest boatman replied.

"We gotta obey the captain's orders on a boat or it's mutiny," another took up defiantly.

"Yes?"

"Yes." This came from several voices.

"Well, let me tell you something. There isn't a man jack of you who does not know perfectly well that the captain's jurisdiction is a very limited one. Your boat was posted with orders every one of you could read, and you were told to remain aboard until I sent for you, or gave you sailing orders. Isn't that so?"

"Yes," one of the men at the back admitted reluctantly.

"Slim!" called Wat.

"Right here." Slim answered.

"Have some of the boys put these fellows in irons, and you'd better leave two or three to swab deck and mend the furniture."

"Right-O. Want them aboard the ship or here?"

"On the island," Wat answered after a moment's hesitation. Then he heaved the unconscious body of the captain through the door to be dragged out by some of Slim's company. Slim gave sharp orders.

"Round em up an' rope em, then, forward march," the young fellow ordered with a mixture of soldier and cowboy.

"We can't march the captain, Slim."

"Leave somebody to guard him while you get a stretcher," Slim replied as if he was getting a great deal of satisfaction out of his job at that particular moment.

"Are you hurt, Miss Langwell?" Wat asked and his voice still sounded as if he was in command of a company.

"No, I'm not, thank you," she said with a sob, which she promptly smothered. "Oh, oh, I'm so glad you came—I never saw anything so ghastly—"

"I hope you never do again," he told her quietly. "But, I want the truth. You are really not hurt, the fighters didn't touch you, or that bunk injure you? Don't be afraid, let Nomie take care of you if you are not perfectly O.K."

"I am perfectly all right," she assured him.

"Good," he gave a little sigh of relief then snapped again: "Slim."

"Coming," shouted Slim.

"Take Miss Langwell out and walk with her along the beach. The fog isn't so bad now and the fresh air will help her recover quickly. Are the rest of the men on the job?"

"Yes, sir, everyone."

"Let me walk with Mr. Slim too," Natell begged as she bobbed up from somewhere.

"If your mother doesn't need you," Wat smiled at the little girl. "You've been a great kid tonight, and the next boat that comes in is going to bring something mighty nice for you."

"You bet," Slim added with a grin. "That boat will have two nice things for you. I'll get my sister to buy you something dandy."

"Good," Nomie nodded, so Natell joined the pair as they made their way out onto the beach. A bucket brigade was already marching toward the door with brimming pails of water to "swab deck."

"Did Natell go for you?" Roberta asked. She was thinking of how the little girl had disappeared among the draperies just before the arrival of the boatmen.

"Sure she did, and how!" Slim answered unsuspectingly, then his companion knew that there was at least two ways of getting in and out of the Indian woman's home, and she resolved that sometime she would explore it if she were ever left alone.

"In my luggage I have some strings of colored beads," the white girl went on. "They are not much, just sort of attractive. You must let me give her some of them right away because it will be a long time before you and Wat can get your presents here, won't it?"

"Be a few weeks," Slim admitted cautiously. "Sure, give her some of yours if you like. Can't be any objection to that."

"All right, Natell, tomorrow you shall have a nice long string of red beads, the prettiest ones I have."

"Good," the girl replied softly, apparently understanding that Roberta had overcome the necessity for secrecy regarding the string she already had.

"If you like one of the others, you may have two strings," Roberta added, no end relieved that the matter of the gift was so simply settled.

"Better walk carefully here," Slim warned, as he changed places with her so that she was on the inside of the beach. "Sort of treacherous at night; beastly in the fog."

"It feels good to be out," Roberta told him as they went on. For half an hour they walked, saying little, until the density of the mist began to chill the white girl, then they returned to the dugout, which except for the wetness of the recent "swabbing," and strips of new boards nailed over the broken furniture, looked exactly as it had before the invasion of the belligerent captain. They found Wat smoking thoughtfully before the door, and after bidding the women good-night, the two men strode off into the darkness. The walk had tired her, so Roberta was really glad to go to bed and in spite of the horrors of the night, she soon dropped off into a sound sleep. When she awakened in the morning, the two Indians were already busy with some task, and Nomie lost no time in preparing food for her charge.

"Go fishing," she informed Roberta when the meal was finished, so, after adding a string of blue beads to the red ones Natell was proudly showing that morning, and adding a storm coat to her costume, the girl Sky-Pilot followed the women out into the sunlight, for every bit of fog had been dispelled. They cut across the island toward the northwest and on a smooth little cove, tugged a deep canoe, which certainly had not been there the day before when the white girl did her exploring.

"The island must be full of hiding places," she remarked to herself, and wondered how much it concealed. By that time Roberta was so full of the mystery of the place that being marooned or imprisoned there was receding further back in her brain; although nothing could make her forget the anxiety she knew must weigh down her own home in far away Long Island, but she determined that if she ever succeeded in getting away, she would be able to give some real information as to what enterprise was conducted there. She thought of Mr. Howe, and then it occurred to her that she was to have had a mission with him. "It couldn't have been more exciting than this thing I've stumbled, or been piloted into."

"Sit here." Nomie designated with a nod a thin cushion in the middle of the boat, which reminded the white girl of pictures she had seen of native-made crafts. She took her place cautiously, for it looked as if it would take very little to turn the thing over, but Natell hopped in one end, then with a short paddle held the boat steady until her mother was safely in the other. Without a word the pair dipped their paddles and the canoe shot speedily over the water, going toward the northwest.

"Little island, much fish," Nomie remarked and Roberta didn't know whether she was speaking of the land they were leaving behind, or another one.

"Is that so," she replied, and Nomie, who was facing her, nodded.

They sped along over the blue water, occasionally pausing to drop a line, and once the Indian woman set a trawler which glistened as it dragged yards behind them. Natell seemed to keep an eye on this, but nothing was caught, and after an hour they reached another island, almost as barren as the one they had left. They sent the boat slowly in and out among jagged rocks and the white girl marveled that they were not dashed against the sharp edges which protruded dangerously all about them.

"Like go shore?" Nomie asked. "Nice shells. Tide going down."

"That will be fine," Roberta agreed readily, so the canoe's nose was shot into an opening between two great wall-like cliffs which looked as if at one time it had been a solid mass. The woman steadied the boat while the girl climbed ashore, and Natell pointed to a series of shelves.

"Climb to top easy," she smiled.

"Shout if tired. We call when ready," Nomie added to the directions, when at last they were ready to pull off. "Take care."

"Thank you," Roberta answered. She wasn't particularly interested in the island, but she was mighty grateful at the opportunity to be alone for a while. She hoped that in the solitude some practical plan would present itself, and she also wondered if this fishing expedition had been gotten up in order to get her out of the way. She recalled that something had been said the night before about a "load" for the captain's boat, so perhaps Wat did not want an audience while this was going on. Then she remembered that she had not caught sight of the vessel, but she hadn't thought of it that morning, so she had not looked. It was doubtless lying-to out beyond the shallow water.

Accepting Natell's suggestion, Roberta climbed to the top of the cliff, which was not very high, then wandered about aimlessly until she came to a long point of wide flat rock which was scarcely above the water. Here she saw quite a collection of brightly colored shells, and as the tide was going out, she started to gather a few of them. Paying little attention to how many steps she took, she went on and on until her hands were full, then glancing up, she saw a short distance ahead was another island, smaller than the one she was on, and the great ledge appeared to join on it. The second island was dense with timber, whose dark green was a great relief after the monotony of sea, sky and white sands, so, watching her step she proceeded and presently was standing under the wide spreading branches of a grove of scrub evergreen.

"Now I appreciate trees more than I ever did before." Glancing back at the ledge, which the dropping tide revealed more and more, she felt it safe to proceed and thoroughly enjoy the wonderful treat. Some places she couldn't get through at all, but for several minutes she proceeded inland, then, suddenly she stopped, stared, rubbed her eyes and looked again, for well concealed in the underbrush, but unmistakable, was a tip of an airplane wing. Her first thought was that some pilot had been brought down and she parted the brush to investigate.

"Reach for the sky, you, and don't turn around!" The command was snapped out sharply and Roberta's hands went over her head without delay.

CHAPTER XII
A SECOND CAPTIVE

"Keep 'em up."

Roberta's heart hammered, but she misunderstood the last part of the order, and faced about quickly.

"Say, what are you doing; I told you not to turn around!"

"I'm not," Roberta retorted.

"You're—say, you're a girl!" A decidedly unkempt looking young man, with nothing more deadly in his hands than a knotted stick, came toward her quickly. "You look like Langwell, the Lurtiss kid pilot."

"I am Roberta Langwell and I'm not a kid," she replied indignantly as she dropped her hands.

"Sure, I saw you when you were touring with the Wallaces. What the— that is, I mean, what are you doing up here?" His hand went to his collar as if to adjust his tie, but there was none there, and a look of dismay spread over his bewhiskered features. "My name's Arnold, but I'm no relation to the guy who tried to betray his country."

"I am a prisoner, Mr. Arnold," she told him.

"You look it. Tell me another," he answered.

"Just the same, that's the truth," she replied, and then, as there was a stump handy, she sat down. "Please don't let me keep you standing. Are we in the Bering Sea?" Arnold sat down with a chuckle.

"The island is," he told her.

"What islands are they, I mean, what are their names?"

"Don't believe these have any because they are not very large, but they belong to the Pribilof group. I believe this is the farthest north and it's a bit over three hundred miles to Alaska."

"Thanks," she said with a sigh. "It's mighty nice to know where one is at. I was piloting for a woman called Pollzoff; and she fed me some kind of dope that knocked me out, then tied me up like a chicken ready to roast, and brought me to an island below here."

"Pollzoff?"

"Yes."

"Go on and tell me the rest." There was no doubt in his tone or manner now.

"Guess I'm what is called kidnaped," Roberta began, then told him quickly all that had happened to her right up to that moment.

"You certainly have been having a terrible time," he remarked soberly. "What was that spring thing in your plane?"

"It's an invention of Mr. Wallace's and I really cannot tell much about it except that it's tuned with the radio stations' broadcasting band and when it is open, if the signal is investigated, Nike can be located."

"That's rich! And Pollzoff went off in your plane; flying right into the arms of the police looking for you. Wish I could see the performance."

"I don't believe she will do anything so stupid as fly into anyone's arms, but just the same, they can find out where Nike goes, that is, if the thing works. Now, tell me, what are you doing here?"

"Sort of a prisoner myself," he answered.

"Oh, did somebody catch you?"

"In a way, yes. I was one of the war air-kids, and after that didn't want to do anything but fly, but the woods were full of fellows trying to do the same thing and the jobs were almost as few and far apart as hen's teeth. Well, I grubbed around like a ground-hog at a desk I finally landed until I saved enough money to buy a plane."

"Yes," Roberta was intensely interested.

"That was before Col. Lindbergh made the air a place for Americans to fly in and while I hopped about, here, there and several other places I wasn't exactly a bright and shining success. Then one day I answered an advertisement I read in a middle west paper and took off on a job that seemed too good to be true. As they told me I would be working for a chain of business firms, I swallowed it hook, line and sinker, with the pole and reel thrown in, and didn't think anything of it when I carried males and females all over the map. I figured they were members of boards, big business stuff with headquarters scattered." He paused again and frowned.

"I see," the girl encouraged.

"I'd been with them a year, and had a real roll in the bank before I made my first trip to Alaska with any of them. It was six months after that before I went over to the Pribilof Islands—"

"Is that where we are?"

"Yes, but not the main ones. They are a bit further south, but these little fellows I guess are all on the same range, like an underseas chain of mountains," he answered, then went on. "I carried mail, supplies and stuff back and forth between them and the mainland, sometimes down to the Aleutian Islands. The Indian woman you call Nomie is an Aleut."

"I wondered."

"That's what she is. Her husband was a seal fisher and got killed when the kid was little. They had the dugout and lived where you're being held so she stayed and worked for the gang, she nurses them when they get sick, and all that sort of thing."

"She's been mighty nice to me," Roberta said quickly.

"She's a darned good Indian and she had to make her living somehow, same as a lot of the rest of us."

"Of course," Roberta agreed.

"At first I hopped on Nomie's island and hopped off again within an hour. Sometimes I took a bale of furs that I thought the other Indians had left there to be sold in the States or Canada. Gee—this story is stretching out and we gotta remember that tide."

"It was going down," Roberta told him.

"Yes, I know it. Well then I began to make longer stops and carry bigger loads, and after a while I happened to pick up a magazine with an article and pictures of the Pribilofs. It told about the seal fishing, how there used to be thousands of the beasts killed every year even at mating time. The United States bought the islands from Russia along with Alaska in 1867 and made laws to prevent the seals being exterminated. Before the war, 1911 I think it was, the United States, Japan, Great Britain and Russia made a treaty agreeing that the white men were not to do any more seal slaughtering. The Indians, because they don't do it in such wholesale lots and because it means the only means of living to a great many of them, are the only people who can kill the migrating seals. They have to do it in canoes with spears or harpoons, can't use guns or motor boats. It was a mighty interesting article, told how the seals start up in pairs from all over the country to raise their young ones."

"Why sure, there's a wonderful story Rudyard Kipling wrote called The White Seal. My mother read it to me when I was a kid, and I always loved it. The White Seal went to an Island called St. Paul's."

"That's it. I liked that story too. Well, I knew radio as well as flying, so by and by I had to relieve the regular chap at that."

"I've wondered if they have a radio."

"They have, but it isn't much of one. It's just used for signals. While I was doing that I discovered that when the seals came up in April and all through the summer, a bunch of them were run through a sort of pen and killed. There aren't as many of them coming up now as there used to be but the gang goes after them any old way and slaughters two hundred times more than the Indians bring in every season. It was while I was there that Wat was put in charge. I figured he was in the same boat with me; that he had been working for them for a long time before they let him get hep to what was going on, then they'd sunk him so deep he couldn't do anything but hang on; besides he's got a kid sister in Saranac trying to get a permanent T. B. cure and that costs a lot of money. I know because he asked me to drop down there one time and pay the bill—it was some bill, and I saw the kid, she's only about thirteen years old."

"That's too bad," Roberta said.

"Sure. Well, I'm free, white, and twenty-one, and when I figured I was signed up with a bunch of crooks I made up my mind to quit. I got a full-sized fondness for my Uncle Sam, been batting about other countries a lot, so while I don't think the United States hasn't room for improvement, it suits me right down to the ground, and I haven't any hankering to end my brilliant career in a Federal prison while the guy I work for stays hidden and lets me hold the bag. First I thought Pollzoff was the head of the thing, then I heard Wat tell her where to get off at a couple of times for not obeying orders, but she's got some money invested in the business so does somewhat as she pleases."

"I wish she hadn't picked on me," Roberta said ruefully.

"She got everlastingly sore when she could not get a license, and I figure, from what you say, that while she was flying around with you, she got jealous because you landed what she couldn't. When a woman of her type gets jealous, she's deadlier than a whole herd of males. Probably they planned to get you to work for them as a sort of blind, but she couldn't wait, and shoved the works hard. Anyway, when I made up my mind to quit, I knew I had to do it mighty carefully. I wasn't leaving Nomie's very often then and it wasn't easy, but finally one day I started off in the plane, that was about six weeks ago, but they must have been wise. Wat wasn't there that day and the fellow in charge had the machine gun turned on me before I could get very high. The shot ripped off my tail but I gave the bus the gas and went on just the same. Couldn't do a very good job of steering, and it was foggy, so this is as far as I got. Now, you know all about me." He stared ahead with a scowl.

"My goodness, how have you managed to live? Were you hurt when you came down?"

"Hurt some, sure, but not bad. Got a crack on my head that seems to have affected my eyes. Then I discovered a vessel wrecked off the other side and managed to salvage her stores. Hunted for some of the crew but none of them got as far as the island, I guess. Been trying to fix up the bird again, but it's been slow work and I've been wondering if I can fly her when she is finally fixed."

"Well, if you can't," Roberta said eagerly, "I can."

"By Jove, that's so. Tell you what, you go back with Nomie and come here again. Know how to paddle a canoe?"

"A little, but I could never manage one of the native boats."

"Get Natell to teach you. Take advantage of everything you can while you're stranded. The whole country will be looking for you by this time, and they won't stop. Nobody knows I disappeared, but maybe when they get you out, someone will help me."

"Of course they will. Do you think I'll go off without you?" Roberta demanded indignantly. Wasn't he a fellow pilot in distress? "And, when we get to the United States you can have your eyes attended to and they'll be all right again."

"Say, funny thing. I've heard about you in a lot of different places and from different people, and the same phrase popped into my head that I've heard about you. They all say, you're a great kid, but," he added hastily, "They don't mean that you're a baby, or anything like that; and I don't either, you know what I mean."

"Sure," she agreed heartily.

"Now, while we've been talking, I've got a sort of plan."

"What is it?"

"You go back with Nomie. Don't say a word about seeing me, and come with her again as often as she'll fetch you. Perhaps they'll let you have a little boat. I can't put up any kind of signal for I don't want them to spot me before I'm ready to take off. You don't do any more snooping around because I know the whole works and you might get into further difficulties. Just keep your eyes open ordinarily and wait. I'll look around for you every day and see you when you are coming this way, then if you have any news you can tell me, and if I think of anything more, I can tell you. I'll go on, finishing the plane, and if we don't get away before that's ready, we can make a plan to give them the slip. There was a small boat on that vessel and I've got it hauled up under some weeds; haven't thought of using it, but we may be glad to have it," he proposed eagerly and Roberta was intensely interested.

"That's a corking plan."

"I don't suppose you have any of your instruments."

"They are all in Nike."

"I have a pocket compass off the ship, a real good one. You take it back with you and keep it out of sight. If you should come alone, it will help you." He gave her the highly sensitive instrument and after examining it carefully, she dropped it into the pocket of her blouse.

"May I see the plane?"

"Sure." He swept an armful of boughs and sand off the machine showing that he had not only been working on the plane, but had cleared a take-off space which he covered again. "Nomie and Natell come up around the other end of these twin islands for fish and wood a couple of times a week, but neither have been over here yet. You're my first caller and I guess I didn't give you a very polite reception." He noticed that the girl, although she made a hasty examination of the plane, seemed to see every detail.

"Your reception was all right and the bus looks great. It's a wonder to me that you didn't have more of a crack-up than you did when you came down."

"I tried my darndest to save the pieces," he grinned.

"And you've got these parts fixed evenly. Why you're doing a bang-up job. Did you find tools on the vessel?"

"Sure, a whole load of them in the carpenter's outfit. Don't know where the tub came from, her name was scraped off, but I surely thanked Providence for depositing the boat right here. There is still some of her left. Perhaps, next time you come you can go around and see what's left of her if the sea doesn't bang her up."

"I should like to very much," Roberta answered, then went on a bit anxiously. "Guess I'd better not linger too long now or Nomie might take it into her head to come looking for me. Now that we've talked over the plan I won't try to do any investigating. I suppose that crack I saw and the noise I heard is the place where the seals are driven and killed."

"That's right, it is, although the seals do not come up in any great numbers any more. Be mighty careful to let them all think over there that you haven't any interest in what they are doing. Wat's pretty decent, as decent as he can be, but he's only one. He and Slim are in a bad crowd of rough-necks. You had a sample of that last night, so be careful," he urged.

"I will," she promised. "It's much easier now that I know where I am located and something about the place. Wonder who the big Boss of the whole thing is?"

"So do I, but the information we have may help in catching the Chief Mogul himself."

"We'll hope so."

"You know, that stranded vessel sounds mighty mysterious to me."

"She is mysterious, but I've been so busy with my own troubles I haven't given her very much thought. I'll see what I can learn from what is left of her. Perhaps we can solve that mystery too, since we've gone into the business," he laughed.

"I'll trot along. If Nomie brings me this way again, or I can come alone, how will I find you, by coming around here?" she asked.

"If I see that you are alone I'll come down to the beach or one of the coves and meet you," he replied. "I'll come with you now to the ledge and see that you get over all right. You don't want to slide off into the Bering. It's cold and wet all the way to the bottom, and that's a good mile."

Presently the two had reached the ledge, found the water a foot lower than when she crossed earlier, so she hurried forward while he watched closely, ready to spring at the first sign of danger, but she reached the other side safely.

"I hear Natell," she called back to him. "So long!"

"S'long, Sky-Pilot," he answered.

Roberta ran as fast as she could to the nearest point and saw the canoe moving swiftly toward the end of the island, but when the Indians sighted her, they paddled more slowly. The white girl, in her trim aviation suit stood an instant outlined against the blue sky as she paused to glance back toward the wooded island where she saw Arnold outlined dimly against the dark green of the forest behind him, then she hurried toward the bit of beach where Nomie and Natell waited.

Riding back from the twin-islands to Nomie's in the bottom of the native canoe, Roberta's heart beat confidently and she felt that her guardian angel had certainly been more than careful of her welfare, but it was mighty difficult to hold her face straight, her lips from smiling complacently or joyously. She managed to control herself, to keep her mouth from betraying her, and it was not difficult to either drop her lids or gaze out over the dancing waters of Bering Sea. It was great to know where she was and she resolved to follow Arnold's instructions to the letter and make no move which would arouse the suspicions of the men on the island. She would avoid being more than ordinarily interested in her surroundings, and at least appear not to be too observant of what went on around her.

The white girl sighed with relief when she saw the desolate island loom up suddenly, looking for all the world as if not a living soul ever went within miles of it.

Presently the canoe shot into a cove and Nomie nodded for her to land, so, while they steadied the boat, she stepped ashore. Immediately the women bent to the oars again and in a few minutes disappeared from sight around a long point of land. Roberta sat down, making the best picture of disconsolation that she could, but with her face hidden between her knees, she could indulge herself in a first class relaxation of her features, and she smiled broadly. Why shouldn't she!

Arnold would get the plane ready in record time, she would go over to twin-islands another day, and they would fly away. It was merely a matter of a short wait and in the meantime she would have a rather jolly experience living with the Indian woman and her daughter; furthermore, the seals promised no end of entertainment.

"I am going to have a real good time," she told herself. "This isn't a half bad place, and I wager I am the first white girl to visit it, which will be something to tell the newspaper reporters when I get home." Just then Natell appeared and beckoned with her finger and Roberta followed to see what was wanted.

Natell lead the way around the opposite end of the island to a huge flat section. Here she paused and motioned Roberta to remain perfectly still. For about two minutes she did, then, a little way out, she saw a pair of dark eyes staring at her, and a moment later, a young seal hauled himself to the land and started in her direction. He came quite close, within four feet, then stopped again, but just then some one of his family called him, and he returned to the water. When he was gone, Natell crept cautiously forward among the rocks, then, with a movement like lightning, she reached down and came up again with a tiny seal in her arms. He whined pitifully, but his curiosity was greater than his fear, so he gave her a sniff.

"Oh, the cunning little fellow," Roberta exclaimed. She petted the baby, but about ten minutes later there was another bark from the water and the young seal flapped comically in front of her. He was so funny that she threw back her head and laughed heartily, she couldn't help it, but it scared the little fellow and he scrambled away. "Next time I must be more polite when I have company," she told herself.

THE END

9 781774 818107